"I don't know how to thank you."

Mitch cocked his head. "Do you have any idea how much fun I've had all day? If you want to know the truth, I felt just like your son. When you said it was time to go home, I didn't want it to end, either."

That makes three, Heidi thought.

Mitch was getting to her in ways she was scared to examine. He was a P.I. whose firm had been hired to find out what was going on at her company. But already he was coming to mean much more.

"What can I do to help you tomorrow?"

"Anything you'd like. Just don't go near your office or the plant. After I've gone in the facility to install the devices, I'll phone you and we'll go from there. Expect a call around two."

He turned to leave, then looked back over his broad shoulder. His eyes appeared black in the  "For what it's worth, I think your ex-husba have been out of his mind to let you and away from him."

Mitch shouldn't have told her that. Partic she knew he'd be leaving Salt Lake soon.

Dear Reader,

Up by the University of Utah where I lived and went to college, there was a wonderful place to get a snack and drinks. It was called The Spudnut Shop. Everyone used to go there. The place was terribly popular because of the unique recipe of the doughnuts.

For a while I dated the son of the man who owned the franchise. Of course when he first asked me out (we were in a college class together), I had no idea of his relationship to the owner. For one thing, he was from California, not a local guy.

You can't imagine how surprised (and delighted) I was when after going to a movie, he took me there. It was closed, but with a mysterious smile, he used a key to let us in. It was so much fun to be waited on by him. He turned on the radio and served us those famous spudnuts and root beer. Talk about exciting, with just the two of us in the shop where I'd been many times with my high school and college friends.

Sadly the shop eventually closed. Years later I was watching a documentary on the highlights of old Salt Lake and was reminded of it again. I got thinking about what a romantic date that had been, and suddenly the idea for a new novel came to mind, *The Marshal's Prize*.

Enjoy!

Rebecca Winters

The Marshal's Prize

REBECCA WINTERS

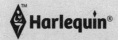

TORONTO NEW YORK LONDON
AMSTERDAM PARIS SYDNEY HAMBURG
STOCKHOLM ATHENS TOKYO MILAN MADRID
PRAGUE WARSAW BUDAPEST AUCKLAND

Recycling programs
for this product may
not exist in your area.

ISBN-13: 978-0-373-75402-1

THE MARSHAL'S PRIZE

ABOUT THE AUTHOR

Rebecca Winters, whose family of four children has now swelled to include five beautiful grandchildren, lives in Salt Lake City, Utah, in the land of the Rocky Mountains. With canyons and high alpine meadows full of wildflowers, she never runs out of places to explore. They, plus her favorite vacation spots in Europe, often end up as backgrounds for her romance novels, because writing is her passion, along with her family and church. Rebecca loves to hear from readers. If you wish to email her, please visit her website, www.cleanromances.com.

Books by Rebecca Winters

HARLEQUIN AMERICAN ROMANCE

1261—THE CHIEF RANGER
1275—THE RANGER'S SECRET
1302—A MOTHER'S WEDDING DAY
     "A Mother's Secret"
1310—WALKER: THE RODEO LEGEND
1331—SANTA IN A STETSON
1339—THE BACHELOR RANGER
1367—RANGER DADDY
1377—A TEXAS RANGER'S CHRISTMAS
1386—THE SEAL'S PROMISE *

*Undercover Heroes

HARLEQUIN ROMANCE

4148—CINDERELLA ON HIS DOORSTEP
4172—MIRACLE FOR THE GIRL NEXT DOOR
4185—DOORSTEP TWINS
4191—ACCIDENTALLY PREGNANT!
4219—THE NANNY AND THE CEO
4239—HER DESERT PRINCE
4244—AND BABY MAKES THREE
     "Adopted Baby, Convenient Wife"
4271—HER ITALIAN SOLDIER
4291—A BRIDE FOR THE ISLAND PRINCE

To my terrific editor, Kathleen Scheibling,
who believes in me and my ideas. I'm very lucky.
Every author should have the privilege.

Chapter One

"Your rotary cuff has healed, Mitch. You have one hundred percent mobility and are cleared to return to work full-time. Today I'll have the office fax the information to your superior, Lew Davies, in Florida. After being away from your job almost a year, I'm sure he'll be happy to get you back on active duty."

No doubt about it. Lew Davies, more like a father figure to Mitch in the past year, would be ecstatic at the news. He needed Mitch on the job yesterday. That was a given.

"Thank you, Dr. Samuels," he said. "I appreciate all that you and the staff have done for me."

"You worked hard on your physical therapy and it really shows. Remember, you can get some plastic surgery done on the scars if you feel it's necessary. I guess you know how lucky you are to still have a great future ahead of you."

"I do."

"Take care."

After they shook hands, Federal Marshal Mitchell Garrett walked out of the Orthopedic Specialty Hospital, better known as TOSH, in Salt Lake City, Utah. TOSH was one of the finest facilities for his type of injury in the world, which was why Lew had arranged for him to be flown from Florida to Utah eleven months ago for surgery.

You know how lucky you are to still have a great future ahead of you. As he climbed into his used Audi, Mitch knew how fortunate he was to have fully recovered. Having the full use of his right arm again was his "get out of jail free" card. For during that nightmarish week after his surgery when he went crazy from total inactivity, he'd felt as though he'd been thrown in jail. Lew knew how Mitch had felt. To make certain he didn't climb the walls during the long recuperation period, he'd arranged temporary work for Mitch at the Roman Lufka Private Investigators firm in Salt Lake.

Lew had maintained that a P.I. job would be a less hostile work environment for Mitch, yet still keep his brain revved. It was a feasible solution for the off time while he trained the muscles in his arm and shoulder to function properly again.

Mitch had liked Roman Lufka from the start. The man was a total professional. It didn't take long to understand why Lufka's firm was recognized as the best P.I. firm in the Intermountain West. To his surprise Mitch found he enjoyed the work there, too. The cases were varied and challenging. Better yet, he didn't have to watch his back every second, the way he did as a marshal.

As a result he found more time to make friends with the office staff, especially a couple of the P.I.s, Chaz and Travis. Like Mitch, they'd both come from military and law-enforcement backgrounds. Chaz, who'd lost his wife to cancer, had recently married again and was now a stepfather to a cute little girl. Travis had been with the Texas Rangers until his wife was murdered in a revenge killing. He'd resigned and brought his son to Salt Lake, where he could have the support of his sister's family.

Mitch had come close to marriage several times, but he had a tendency to be somewhat of a loner and liked his own space. Because he didn't crave doing things as a couple all the time, the women he'd gotten close to felt it reflected on them and the relationships fizzled out. Though Lew argued with him to the contrary, Mitch was getting to the point where he didn't believe marriage was for him. He'd dated several women lately, but felt no spark.

Now that eleven months had passed and he was fit to resume his duties as a federal marshal, he felt conflicted.

To be conflicted was a state of mind he'd never experienced and didn't understand, because until this point in his life he'd always known exactly what he wanted to do and had felt good about his decisions. He should be excited and happy to know he could get back to his career in Florida. But he wasn't and it disturbed him.

After he turned on the Audi's ignition, he drove to his apartment, near the University of Utah. Though he should phone Lew and tell him the news, he wasn't ready to do that yet. What he needed right now was coffee. It wouldn't help his nerves, but he craved the caffeine.

When he wheeled into the double carport he shared with a pair of female college students in the next apartment, he saw the mailman chatting with them. They loved to party and were probably hitting on the guy.

Not wanting to have to turn down their dozenth invitation to hook up, Mitch remained in the car, put his cell phone to his ear and pretended he was deep in conversation. To his relief the girls finally went back into their apartment.

He got out of the car, then grabbed the mail out of the box and hurriedly unlocked the door into his kitchen. He was looking for a letter from the Florida Bureau of Vital Statistics. He wanted any information he could get in the course of his ongoing search for his birth parents.

Over the years, he'd sent the bureau numerous inquiries. Each time he'd hoped the bureau would find a new name to add to the list they'd compiled and sent to him. When he saw the envelope, he felt a rush of adrenaline and tossed the rest of the mail on the counter so he could open it.

Dear Mr. Garrett, in regard to your letter of June 30—the following birth records on those individuals with the last name Garrett, taken from the dates you specified, appear below. If this doesn't help, we suggest you search out every church in the Tallahassee area. They'll have baptismal and christening records. Don't forget the local hospitals, which keep thorough records.

Mitch had already made an attempt to do all the things suggested, but because the nature of his work left him little leisure time, his attempts were sporadic and he couldn't provide the follow-through. An in-depth investigation required months of work without interruption, a luxury he didn't have.

> *As a last resort, you might hire a genealogist.*
> *This can be expensive, but some of the profes-*
> *sionals have done years of work on certain lines*
> *and can be of significant help. The best of luck*
> *to you.*

Mitch appreciated the information. That was one angle he hadn't pursued. While it was on his mind, he sat down at his kitchen table and looked up genealogists in Florida on his laptop. He came across a website for the Florida chapter of the Association of Professional Genealogists. That would be a good place to start, but not right now. He was too restless and had other things to do.

Once he'd rifled through the bills and ads on the counter, he walked into the living room and turned on the TV to see who'd won the most recent stage of the Tour de France. Mitch had done a lot of cycling before his injury. He'd found it relaxing. Right now he was rooting for the American team, but it was the Belgian who won the yellow jersey today. He turned the TV off and went back to the kitchen to make some instant coffee.

While he waited for water to heat in the microwave, he checked his watch. It was 10:00 a.m. He ought to be hungry, but his appetite had deserted him. Once he'd made the coffee, he sweetened it and wandered out onto the veranda. He never tired of the view.

The small apartment for college students he rented was simply a place to sleep while he'd been recuperating. Lew had arranged for him to stay here where he could keep a low profile. Mitch preferred lots of space and the miniscule rooms provided little, but the sight of Salt Lake from this spot made up for it.

Before he'd come to Utah, he'd heard about the Valley of the Great Salt Lake. It was flanked by the Wasatch Mountains on the east and the Oquirrhs on the west, names that came from the Goshute and Paiute Indians respectively. The sight of both ranges rising close to eleven thousand feet in the dry air took his breath every time.

A unique part of the country, Salt Lake. When storms did roll in, they grew into cloudbursts at colossal heights with lightning and thunder that rocked the whole region. Right now there wasn't a cloud in the sky. It was hot already. By this afternoon the temperature would reach one hundred again, typical for mid-July.

Being a Florida native, he was used to the heat. In Florida, in fact, the heat was made more intense by the humidity. If he had to choose between both places to live and work in the U.S., the West and Salt Lake would probably win out. *Except...* Whether rational or not, Mitch didn't know if he could leave Florida for good. The sooner he contacted a genealogist in the area, the better.

He swallowed the last of his coffee. Tomorrow he'd phone Lew, who would have received the fax from Dr. Samuels. In the meantime Mitch needed to get to the P.I. office. He'd finally nabbed the culprits in the mail-fraud case he'd been working on, and there was paperwork to finish up. Anything would be better than staying here and dwelling on this new freedom, which had brought him to a crossroads he wasn't ready for. Mitch would wait until the end of the day to tell Roman his sick leave was up.

THE SECOND HEIDI BAUER NORRIS walked into her office at Bauer's Incorporated after her lunch break, the phone rang. She was the director of human resources for the company that made SweetSpud Donuts, and Mondays were always like this for her. You didn't have time to catch your breath before everything over the weekend that could go wrong came to light. She dashed to her desk and picked up the receiver on her extension. "This is Heidi."

"I'm glad you answered. It's Phyllis from No. 2."

Bauer's had twenty donut shops in the Salt Lake Valley. Heidi knew them by number. "Yes, Phyllis. How's your daughter?"

"She still has a lot of morning sickness."

"I'm sorry to hear that. I went through those days while I was carrying Zack. Tell her to hang in there and eat soda crackers before she gets out of bed. It works. What can I do for you?"

"Jim didn't come in this morning. His wife just phoned and said he was sick on Saturday so he went to the doctor. It seems he has to go into the hospital for a series of tests to find out what's wrong with his stomach. He'll be out until Thursday. I can handle today without him, but somebody needs to be here for Tuesday and Wednesday."

"I'll take care of it right away and be in touch with you."

She'd barely hung up when her great-uncle Bruno Bauer, the CEO of the family-owned company, rolled into her office. He still had his brains and the energy of ten people, but since the stroke that had left him unable to walk, he'd had to rely on a wheelchair to get around.

Last week he'd started coming into the office in the afternoons. She'd visited him a lot during his recuperation period and knew how much he'd hated the restrictions. At least now he was back at the work he loved.

To her surprise, he closed and locked the door behind him. Intrigued by his action, she crossed the room to hug him. "This is a surprise. Why didn't you ask me to come upstairs?"

He patted her hand. "Because since I've been back, my office is like Grand Central Station. Too many busybodies. Too many ears. I didn't want anyone walking in on us, but no one's going to question my wanting to talk to my favorite Adelheide first."

"So what's up?" she asked. Besides the father she adored, she loved Bruno. He and her grandfather were brothers who'd also been best friends. When her grandfather had died, she'd claimed Bruno as another grandfather. He'd always gone out of his way to be kind to her. After her divorce two years ago, he'd brought her into the home office.

The action had miffed some of the family, who'd questioned his action for their own selfish reasons. She'd been only twenty-seven at the time; they were older and more qualified. But none of them had any idea how he'd helped her restore a little self-worth.

"I phoned your father last night and then spent hours talking to him. Sit down and I'll tell you about it."

Heidi took her place behind the desk while he drew around the side to be close to her. There had to be major trouble for him to call her father, who'd gone on a trip to Nebraska with her mom. They were visiting Heidi's older sister, Evy, who'd just had her third baby.

"What's wrong?"

His eyes, light blue like hers, suggested their Austrian roots, but today the blue seemed to have a grayish tinge. He looked troubled. "I have reason to believe Jonas and Lucas are stealing from the company."

"Oh, no!" Jonas and Lucas were the son and grandson respectively of Bruno's sister Rosaline.

Bruno nodded solemnly and told her what he'd discovered. "In all the years this company has been in business, we've had small thefts here and there, but we've never had anything major like this." He went on to give her the details. "Your father agrees with me we need immediate expert help from an outside source."

"You mean the police."

"No. They'll bungle it." He waved his hand. "I want answers fast in an environment of absolute secrecy. This is where you come in. I've done some checking and want you to go to this P.I. firm today. They're reputed to be the best. I've called them and they'll be expecting you. Talk to the owner. Tell him the problem and find out what he suggests."

He pulled a paper from his suit pocket with a name and address on it and handed it to her. She was surprised to discover it read "Roman Lufka Private Investigators," located on Wasatch Boulevard. She must have passed it thousands of times, but she'd never known anything about it.

Bewildered, she stared at Bruno. "You trust me to take care of something this critical?"

He eyed her steadily. "No one knows the ins and outs of this company better than you do, and your father agrees with me. You're as brainy and savvy as my grandmother Saska, who started the whole thing. One day you'll be the CEO, mark my words."

Not if some of the family had anything to do with it, Heidi thought. Besides, she didn't have aspirations in that regard. But she loved him for saying it. Tears pricked her eyes before she got up from the chair and hugged him again.

Bruno could have asked anyone on the twelve-member board—all family—to do this. They'd had years more experience and wisdom. Yet the fact that he and her father had so much faith in her gave Heidi a much needed morale boost. Her bad choice of husband and ugly divorce had badly undermined her confidence.

"I want you free to work with this firm, so I'm going to ask your aunt Marcia to take over your duties temporarily. I'll tell her you'll be busy for the rest of this week visiting our outlets around the valley. That way no one will suspect anything. I trust you to handle this any way you see fit. This has to be between you and me and your father, no one else."

Though Bruno had bestowed a distinct honor on her, she couldn't help but be troubled. "Do you think Rosaline is behind this?"

He looked agonized. "My sister and I have always been at odds, but I don't think she put Jonas and Lucas up to this. Unfortunately I can't rule it out as a possibility."

She nodded. The Bauers were a huge family with many internal problems. Bruno had put out little fires for years on a regular basis, but Jonas and Lucas stealing from the company was a totally different level of concern.

"Go ahead and leave now," Bruno said. "Phone me tonight and tell me how it went." He patted her hand before wheeling out of the room.

Heidi took care of some emails, then grabbed her purse and headed out to her white Nissan, parked at the side of the building. After dropping her six-year-old son, Zack, off at school earlier in the day, she'd driven to work wondering what new problems she might face. She'd never have entertained the thought of their family being on the brink of an internal war, let alone that Bruno would have put her in charge of working with a P.I. to handle it.

The Bauer building was located just below Wasatch Boulevard on Thirty-third South. She got in her car and headed for the Lufka firm farther north. After she'd done business there, she would find a substitute for Jim. By then it would be time to pick up Zack.

When she entered the P.I. building, the receptionist said they'd been expecting her. She was shown into Roman Lufka's private office. The attractive, dark-haired owner listened and asked questions, then excused himself. "I need to see if the P.I. I want to work with you has arrived at the office yet. Can I get you a coffee while you wait?"

"No, thank you."

MITCH HAD LEFT HIS OFFICE door open. To his surprise Roman walked in and put a cup of coffee on his desk. "Do you have a minute?"

"Sure. Thanks for this." He took a sip. What harm was there in one more dose of caffeine? "I was planning to have a talk with you at the end of the day, but as long as you're here, maybe I should get this over with now."

Roman's brows furrowed. "You saw the doctor this morning. What's the verdict?"

His boss was a straight talker. It was one of the reasons Mitch liked him so much. He deserved straight talk back. Letting out a deep sigh he said, "I'm free to return to Florida."

"That's what I was afraid of. I guess I don't have to tell you no one in this office—and I mean no one— wants to see you go, least of all me. Since your arrival, you've become an invaluable asset to the firm. But much as I'd like to twist your arm and beg you to make this your career, I happen to know Lew Davies has been counting the days until your return. I can only imagine you must be anxious to leave, too."

Mitch shot to his feet. "Hell, Roman—I don't know what I'm feeling right now. I've been in a fog since I left TOSH this morning."

"That doesn't surprise me. You may be a crack federal marshal, but you're also a natural-born P.I. I don't want to lose you. Would you like some advice from a man who's been in your shoes?"

"Of course." Mitch had immense respect for Roman, a man in his midforties who'd done and seen a lot in his life.

"Now that your body has healed, give yourself a

little more time to let the news sink in before you make any decision. In the meantime, I have a new case that might appeal to you. It requires your bloodhound instincts." Roman cocked his head. "I hope you're interested, because if you are, I'll talk to Lew Davies and tell him I need you for a little longer. When you've solved this case, maybe by then you'll know if the federal marshal in you won't let go."

"Bless you for the reprieve, Roman." Mitch felt that an enormous weight had been lifted from his shoulders. "Who's the client?"

His boss's face broke out in a broad smile. "You're going to love it."

Mitch chuckled in spite of the seriousness of the situation. His boss was the best and also one of the biggest teases he knew. "I know you're dying for me to ask why."

Roman nodded. "You're not going to believe it. Every guy in the firm would give his eyeteeth to work on it."

"That good, huh?"

"'Good' doesn't begin to describe it. I'll give you a hint. What could none of us around here live without?"

"Coffee."

"Think what goes with it."

Mitch didn't have to think. "SweetSpuds."

"This is your lucky day. I'll bring her in to meet you."

"Her?"

"Heidi Bauer Norris, twenty-nine and divorced with a six-year-old son." He paused at the door. "She's the great-great-granddaughter of Saska Bauer, who emigrated from Austria to Salt Lake in 1892 and founded the Bauer Donut company. Her family has been making SweetSpuds ever since. They're the premier-selling donut in the western half of the U.S. Our firm has helped keep them in business."

Mitch could vouch for that.

"I've already discussed the fee with her. But you might tell her we'd be happy to negotiate part of it. I'm sure you can think of a way that will please everyone."

Laughter rolled out of Mitch, a much needed release. But it quickly subsided when Roman escorted the woman in question into his office seconds later. She was probably five six. Her tailored blue summer suit with the short-sleeved jacket revealed a trim figure.

When Roman introduced them, he found himself looking into impossibly light blue eyes. Her tiny earrings were crystals of the same, which sparkled from beneath a mop of pale gold curls that he bet had looked that way from childhood.

She was in a word, beautiful.

"It's a pleasure to meet you, Ms. Norris. Please sit down."

"Thank you, Mr. Garrett. I appreciate your being available so quickly."

Roman's narrowed eyes sent him a private message. "I'll leave you two alone to discuss the case."

"Being available goes with this business," he said after his boss departed. "It's the nature of the job. Every client's needs are immediate."

She nodded. "My great-uncle Bruno couldn't get me out of the office fast enough this afternoon to talk to someone from your firm."

"We'll do all we can to help you." He smiled, and

in an effort to make her feel comfortable, said, "I understand you have a six-year-old son. Lucky you."

"Yes. His name is Zack and he's the light of my life."

"I can imagine."

He sat down opposite her. "I'm going to record our conversation. Is that all right with you?"

"Of course, but does anyone ever say no?"

"You'd be surprised."

"Then what do you do?"

"Take handwritten notes, but I have difficulty reading my own writing."

"So do I."

When her heart-shaped mouth curved into a smile, Mitch realized he would have to figure out a way not to stare at her. An attraction like this hadn't happened to him for so long, he felt out of his depth.

His boss had been up to his old tricks when he'd teased him about this being his lucky day. He hadn't just been talking about the donuts.

Before he got started, he drank some of his coffee. "I'm going to ask you a lot of questions. Try to be as explicit and detailed as possible. It will help me get the picture I need."

"I'll try."

"Good. Let's start with your great-uncle Bruno. What's his position in the company?"

"He's been the CEO of Bauer's for forty years."

"That's a long time. What's the reason he suddenly needs a P.I., and why didn't he come himself?"

"Bruno is eighty-seven now and confined to a wheelchair because of a stroke he had six months ago. It's hard for him to go many places, but his mind is still razor-sharp, and his wife, my great-aunt Bernice, still fusses over him. His grandson, Karl Bauer—he's thirty-five—works in lower management and drives him to work and back. On his lunch hour Karl picks up Bruno—Bruno puts in half days at the office—then they both go home together."

Despite recording, Mitch took notes just to keep his eyes averted as much as possible. "I assume you're talking about the Bauer building on Thirty-third South? I've passed it many times."

"Yes. It's our headquarters. When I got back from lunch today, Bruno came to my office and told me in private he fears someone within the company is stealing from us. As I've learned over the years, most businesses can expect a certain amount of theft, but we've never had anything this big or alarming until now."

"Does he always confide in you over a serious matter like this?"

"Well, we've always been close. I think of him as my grandfather now that my real grandfather has passed away. They were brothers and best friends. I spent a lot of time with him while he was recovering from his stroke. He says I remind him of his grandmother Saska, who started the company. There's an old family picture of her at the age of twenty-five. I do look like her and he loved her a lot."

"Obviously he loves and trusts you. Who else has he told?"

"My father, Ernst Bauer. He's sixty-three and the general manager of operations for the company. Right now he's in Nebraska with my mother, Marva. They're visiting my older sister, Evy. She's thirty-two and just had her third child. They won't be back for about five more days."

"What's your position in the company?"

"I'm the director of human resources."

"How long have you worked in that position?"

"Two years."

"So if I wanted a job with your company, I would apply to you."

"Right. I don't have the power to hire, but I make recommendations. So far every prospective employee I've vetted has been hired."

"I'm sure your great-uncle finds that impressive. Do you have any siblings besides Evy?"

"Yes. My brother, Rich. He's thirty-six and has been head of the accounting department for five years. He's married to Sharon and they have four children."

Mitch sat back in his chair. "Explain to me what exactly is being stolen."

"The mix for our donuts. It's manufactured and bagged at our plant in Woods Cross. We ship it all over the western states in our own fleet of trucks. The bags are loaded from the warehouse onto the trucks and they're delivered to our various outlets and franchises."

"How did Bruno discover the theft?"

"Through his closest friend, Victor Tolman. Vic's son Don owns a Bauer donut franchise in Phoenix. Bruno and Vic talk all the time. When he found out Bruno was well enough to get back to work, Vic confided something he'd been holding back.

"It seems that over the last five months, one bag of mix in every shipment arriving in Phoenix was missing. In its place was a bag of potato flour."

Mitch eyed her in puzzlement. "Potato flour?"

"Yes. Our SweetSpuds are made with potato flour rather than wheat. It's from an old recipe Saska brought with her from Austria. When there was no wheat available there, they cooked potatoes, then dried them and crushed them into powder to make their bread. It's the reason our donuts outsell other kinds. Potato flour makes a much lighter donut."

"I had no idea. That's fascinating. I can eat a dozen at one sitting."

She laughed softly. "Bruno would love to hear you say that."

"Do you grow your own potatoes?"

"No. We buy a special kind in Idaho and have them shipped down to our plant. Through a unique process we turn them into flour and put it in bags. They're stored in the Woods Cross facility before being taken to the other part of the plant where the mix is made up and put into bags to be shipped."

"Are all the bags the same?"

"Yes, but they have a different tag. The flour-only tag is red, the mix tag is blue—they're sewn into the bottom seam of each bag and the expiration date for the contents is stamped beneath them. The men loading and unloading the bags on dollies wouldn't notice the color of the tags unless they're looking for it. But they wouldn't be looking because the bags are kept in separate areas and depend on the quality-control person to catch mistakes like that."

"How many locations receive deliveries?"

"Four hundred and thirty. When the mistake happened the first time, Don dismissed it. But it happened again in each of the three subsequent shipments. By the fifth shipment he talked to his father who advised him to email the plant office. Don received an email back telling him his next shipment would contain five extra bags of mix and sorry for the inconvenience.

"When Bruno tried to pull up the emails, they weren't there. Suspecting something was wrong, he phoned the manager of our outlet in Albuquerque and learned the same thing had been happening. The manager had reported the errors by email, and the plant had shipped him an extra bag each time. Again Bruno couldn't find those emails. After another call to one of the franchises in San Bernardino, Bruno heard the same story and came to the conclusion it was happening everywhere."

"What's the shipping frequency?"

"Shipments go out every weekday to all the western states, including Utah. Bruno figures that over the last five months, hundreds of bags of mix have been stolen."

Mitch let out a low whistle. "That's quite a few bags pilfered while Bruno was ill. If unstopped it wouldn't take long to stockpile a nice stash that could be used to sell donuts under another name."

"Exactly," she said. "When Bruno first had his stroke, there was talk that he would never be able to come back to work. But he's a fighter and went to therapy. He put in his first half days last week, yet since his return, neither Jonas—he's the plant manager—nor his son, Lucas, who runs the warehouse, has mentioned there's a problem. He believes one or both of them are covering up."

"Not necessarily. It might be some underlings deleting the emails and pulling this off under their noses."

"You're right. Could be anyone in the warehouse."

"Tell me about Jonas and Lucas."

"Jonas is the son of Bruno's oldest sister, Rosaline Martin. He's sixty-one and the head of the plant. He could be masterminding the thefts through his son, Lucas, who runs the warehouse and is the quality-control person."

"How old's Lucas?"

"Thirty-seven. He has a wife and three children."

"Aside from assuming that greed and/or jealousy could be the motive, plus the fact that these two hold key positions in the company—which give them the means to carry out this crime—is there any other reason Bruno has suspected them particularly?"

"Rosaline has always wanted to expand Bauer's to the Midwest and East Coast. We know she has indoctrinated her children with that idea. Some of the other family members agree with her, but Bruno has never seen the need to grow the company because of the headaches involved. So far there haven't been enough votes for her wishes to prevail at the family board meetings."

"So it's very possible either Jonas or his son, or both, have decided to take things into their own hands," Mitch surmised. She nodded. "Run me through the quality-control process."

"During the workday, the mix is made up and put into bags. A crew of warehouse workers loads them on motorized carts and they're taken to the warehouse bay where they're left overnight, ready to load on trucks the next day. Jonas's job is to count them and put all the information in the computer.

"The next day the bags are loaded on trucks. When

they're filled, the crew boss, Randy Pierson—he's another Bauer—checks off the shipments and stores the information in the computer. Lucas prints out what has been stored in the computer and makes a hard copy, which he leaves in Jonas's in-basket.

"One of the employees working at the outlet or franchise on the receiving end of the delivery helps take the shipment off the truck and sends an email receipt back to Lucas. It shows the itemized list that includes the date, actual hour of delivery and amount of goods delivered.

"But again, the people receiving the goods wouldn't think to look at the tags. All they're concerned about is the correct number of bags arriving. It might be a week or two before the bakers opening a new bag discovered the flour and realized a mistake had been made. Obviously that's what happened in Don's case. It's all very random, so that—"

"So that it looks innocent enough," Mitch broke in. "What's done with the flour?"

"It's disposed of."

"Why not returned?"

"Because the flour we use must be freshly bagged. That's company policy. It can't be used outside the plant and we can't take it back once it has left the plant."

"That means you're not only losing money on all the stolen mix, you're losing revenue from the wasted flour, the cost of the bags, money paid the warehouse workers loading the trucks and flour, money paid the drivers, etc."

"Precisely. If there's anything Bruno hates more than laziness, it's waste."

Mitch's brows lifted. "Guess that's why he's been in charge all these years. No doubt his stroke caused the culprits to believe they were home free. By disposing of the emails, there's no 'paper' trail."

She let out a troubled sigh. "Bruno talked to my father. They want to catch them in the act, whoever it is. That's why Bruno decided to hire a P.I. firm—he wants definite proof before confronting them."

"Your great-uncle sounds like a shrewd man."

"He's brilliant, but he's torn up inside to think members of our own family are doing this. Still, he refuses to see the company suffer under his watch."

"How many are on the board?"

"Twelve."

"Give me the names of the family members who would like to see the company grow."

"Besides Rosaline, my great-aunt Frieda and uncle Ray Owens have been outspoken about it for a long time. Frieda's my grandfather's next oldest sister. When I'm around them, she grumbles about Bruno being too steeped in archaic ideas to run the company any longer. She was upset when I was put in the human resources position instead of her grandson Anthony. But she has two other grandchildren who hold responsible positions—Randy's the crew boss and Nadine runs the operation for the mix."

Mitch steepled his fingers. "Considering the foment going on, I'm impressed your great-uncle has managed to run such a successful enterprise. Tell me—who's the keeper of the flame?"

"You must be talking about the recipe. It's locked in a safe-deposit box at the bank. No one has access to it but the CEO, currently Bruno. It can't be opened without him, the head of the bank and the attorney for the company being present. The various workers only know one part of the recipe. No one knows the whole thing.

"When Bruno retires or dies—" Mitch could see the thought upset her "—a new CEO would have to be chosen before he or she had the right to go to the bank and look at it in the presence of the other two witnesses."

Mitch nodded. "That's the best way to safeguard a secret recipe for famous wine or chocolate these days. But as your great-uncle has found out, no measures are foolproof. Since no one in your family but him can get to the actual recipe, it appears certain members are determined to do it the old-fashioned way. I wouldn't put it past them to hire a chemist to analyze the ingredients and try to duplicate your recipe, but that's a very difficult thing to do."

She shivered. "It's so cold-blooded."

"That's the nature of crime. Clearly it's happening at the warehouse. Do you hire trucks?"

"No. We own a fleet of twenty-two located on the Woods Cross property."

"How many workers total are employed there?"

"Including the drivers, one hundred and ten people. Fourteen are family members who oversee the various divisions within the facility."

"That was going to be my next question. There may be more than two family members involved in the thefts out there."

A pained expression crossed her face before she nodded.

"It's evident they're the total opposite of your ancestor Saska."

"What do you mean?"

"From what you've just told me, she was one of those exceptional pioneers I've heard about who helped forge the West into greatness."

The light blue eyes grew shimmery. "That's exactly what she did."

For a brief moment he felt a tug on his emotions that surprised him. He finished the rest of his coffee while he gathered his thoughts.

"Large families who work together are notorious for having inside problems. I'm sure yours is no different, with its mix of angels and less than angels who, because of ego, greed or dreams of power, want to take shortcuts to success."

A sadness crept over her face. "That describes some of our family members."

"And possibly some nonfamily employees who are being paid off because they want or need the extra cash and feel no particular loyalty to the company or your great-uncle. It happens every day. I'm sorry it's happened to your family's company."

"So am I." Her voice caught. "No one has worked harder than Bruno to keep the company profitable and provide every benefit for the employees."

"Some people are never satisfied. They'll always want more."

"That's true," she whispered. Mitch heard a haunted note in her voice, wondering if she was thinking about something that had nothing to do with her family's business.

"In order to find out what exactly is going on, it'll

be necessary for me to infiltrate. But first I'll need a little hands-on experience in the shortest amount of time before you move me out to the plant. What kind of a job can you give me right now to familiarize myself with the product?"

She was so quiet for a minute, he thought she'd been too deep in thought to hear him.

"Ms. Norris?"

Her eyes finally lifted to his. "The baker at our No. 2 shop will be in the hospital undergoing some tests for a few days. Phyllis, the manager, called me earlier today to ask me to find a replacement. I'll tell her no one was available because they're away on summer vacation. Therefore I was forced to hire a new applicant and will train you myself. We'll start first thing tomorrow morning."

The idea of working with her appealed to Mitch like crazy. "What time?"

"Six? Does that sound awful?"

"No. I'm an early bird. But what about your job at headquarters?"

"Bruno has asked my aunt Marcia, who oversees the insurance department, to cover my position at the office for the rest of the week. She had my job before she was moved to that department and can fill in without problem. He's instructed me to assist you so you can resolve this problem ASAP."

He felt a sudden rush of excitement he couldn't explain. All the time they'd been talking, he'd been wondering how he could get to know her better without seeming too obvious.

"Where's the shop located?"

"At SweetSpuds on Foothill, not far from here."

This was getting better and better. "That's our home away from home during working hours around here. My apartment's near the entrance to Emigration Canyon, maybe two minutes away. The situation couldn't suit me better."

"It suits me, too. My house is in the St. Mary's area near the Foothill shopping center. Zack's school is only two blocks from there. Which reminds me, I have to leave now or I'll be late to pick him up."

"Let me walk you to your car." He got up from his desk and followed her out the door, enjoying the trail of her subtle lemony fragrance. "Is he in a summer school camp?"

"No. It's year-round school. He'll be off track in two weeks. That's when I'll take my vacation to be home with him."

"I see." They went down the hall past Roman's office. His door was closed. Everyone in the office looked busy, but he noticed them casting glances at her. You couldn't help it. He wouldn't be surprised if she stopped traffic when she stepped outside. Lisa Gordon, Roman's married assistant, gave him a secret smile before they went out the front door. She was always trying to interest him and Travis in some terrific single woman she knew.

In a minute he was helping Heidi into her Nissan. "I'm going to need more information from you, but there's no time now. Will you be free to talk on the phone later?"

"I can after I put Zack to bed."

"Will eight-thirty be all right?"

"Yes. He'll be asleep by then."

"If you'll give me your cell phone number, I'll program it in mine right now."

They exchanged phone numbers before she started her car and drove out of the parking area.

Mitch walked back inside the building unable to relate to the man who six hours ago didn't know which foot to put in front of the other. Now would be the time to email Lew and set up a time to discuss his clean bill of health, but he was in the middle of a case. After it was solved, he would call him to discuss future plans.

Chapter Two

Heidi got out of her car and waited by the passenger door for Zack. Her dark-blond first-grader came running over in his shorts and Shrek T-shirt, carrying his backpack. He used to have a head of curls, but when he told her how much he was teased at school, she took him to the barber and he now sported a buzz. In an instant her little boy had disappeared.

While they were still on the school grounds, she couldn't expect a hug and a kiss. The big guys didn't do that. He wanted to be a big guy so badly, he climbed in the backseat and strapped himself in his car seat.

"How was school?"

"Good. Can we get a grape slushie?"

"Sure. It's hot out." She pulled in at a convenience store. Once they were on their way again she said, "What was the favorite thing you did today?"

"Recess." He rarely gave her a different answer. From what she'd learned at the last parent-teacher conference, he was doing well in all his subjects, but needed work on making better letters. "When will Grandma and Grandpa be home?"

"This weekend." But she knew better than to give him an exact time. Heidi realized he was missing them. Though he didn't see them every day, it was the idea that they'd gone far away. They'd always fussed over him. "I thought we'd see if Tim wants to come over for a while."

Her brother, Rich, and his family lived a few blocks away. Though Tim was a year older, Zack liked him a lot and they'd played well together, until recently.

"Can we just go home instead?"

"What's wrong? Are you feeling sick?"

"No. I just want to watch SpongeBob."

He'd been watching quite a bit of TV alone after school lately while Heidi got their dinner ready. "Tim likes that cartoon, too."

Through the rearview mirror she saw Zack shake his head. "All he wants to do is ride his bike."

Ah. Heidi got the picture. Rich had taught Tim how to ride, but Zack still had to rely on training wheels for his bike and he felt stupid around his cousin. She'd tried to help her son, but he cried and got frustrated. He probably didn't want to look like a baby who needed his mother to help him. When Rich tried to offer a suggestion, he said he wanted to go home.

A problem for another day. After she'd divorced Gary, she'd tried to make up for the lack of a father in the home, but it was hard. And of course Rich wasn't Zack's father. A boy wanted his own father.

Zack didn't remember Gary. At the time of the divorce, he'd only been four. Heidi had put some pictures of him on Zack's dresser and the rest in an album she'd put away. Some day he'd want to see them. Gary, who'd worked for her family's company, had been too eager to get ahead fast. She hadn't realized how power hungry he was. Toward the end of their marriage, her father had fired him for getting into too many struggles with his immediate boss.

Among the many things Gary had found wrong with Heidi during their four years together, he'd been furious that she didn't fight to help him keep his job. After the divorce, he only came around one time. Though he'd said it was to see Zack, he'd really shown up to harass her and tell her she'd ruined his life. It didn't surprise her that the first of the court-ordered child support payments didn't arrive. None did.

Heidi made enough money without them and never reported the failure because she wanted nothing more to do with the angry man he'd become. She'd felt nothing but relief when her attorney found out from his attorney that he'd signed away his parental rights and had left Utah. He'd gone back to Oregon where he'd been raised by his grandparents.

Zack had accepted Heidi's explanation that she and his daddy didn't get along and he now lived somewhere else. But the day was fast coming when her son would want more in-depth answers. Just the other day he'd asked how come his uncle Rich and aunt Sharon weren't divorced. Heidi had said that some couples were more compatible. She'd sat down with him to explain the meaning of compatibility. He'd listened, not saying anything before he went to sleep.

While Zack watched cartoons in the family room, Heidi phoned her sister-in-law and made arrangements to drop Zack off at their house early in the morning so she could be at the shop by six. Sharon was the best, and said she would drive him and her children to school later.

With that settled, she fixed dinner. Afterward she

helped Zack with his homework, then he took a bath. Once he'd put on his Transformer pajamas and had said his prayers, she let him pick out a couple of his favorite books and they read together until he fell asleep.

It was quarter to nine and her cell phone hadn't rung yet. To her irritation she'd been anticipating talking to the P.I. since she'd left his office. Maybe he'd had something else come up and couldn't call. Impatient with herself, she walked into the living room and sat down on the couch to phone Bruno. Her great-uncle usually went to bed early, so she thought she'd better make contact now.

He liked what she had to tell him about Mitch and approved of the infiltration idea. Halfway through her conversation with him, she discovered someone was trying to reach her. She told Bruno she'd talk to him tomorrow and clicked off to take the other call.

"Hello?"

"Ms. Norris, it's Mitch Garrett." The male voice she remembered sounded deeper over the phone, curling her toes. "Sorry I'm calling a little late, but it couldn't be helped. If this isn't a convenient time—"

"It's fine. I just got Zack to sleep."

"Then I'm glad I didn't interrupt. Since we need to talk, how would you feel if I dropped by your house? I can be there in a few minutes."

An unexpected feeling of excitement swept through her. "That's fine. I'll watch for you."

After they hung up, she hurried into the bathroom to brush her hair and put on lipstick. She hadn't been out on a date since before she'd met Gary. Not that this was a date or anything like it. Still, Mitch Garrett was a very attractive man. Something about him made her aware of herself as a woman. He probably had that effect on every female he met.

When she saw lights in the driveway, she felt another quickening inside of her. What on earth? He'd come over to discuss this terrible thing happening in the company and here she was waiting for him with this fluttery feeling in her chest.

She opened the door for him. "Come in."

"Thank you." The minute he stepped into the living room of her house, he noticed the stand-up framed photo of Zack and paused to look at it.

"Your son looks amazingly like you, but he's darker blond and his eyes are a deeper blue." Mitch managed to notice everything. "He even has your curly hair."

"He did until recently when I took him for a haircut. Zack told the barber to make him look like a Marine."

Mitch chuckled. "Every boy his age wants to look like a man. With a tough name like Zack, he's got to fit the part. Did you cry when he was sheared?"

Heidi laughed. For that kind of understanding she supposed he was married with a family, even if he didn't wear a wedding band. "Yes, I shed a few tears while he wasn't looking."

"Just remember he's cooler this way."

"I'm sure that's true."

Mitch walked around, studying the rest of the family pictures, nodding when she told him who he was looking at. "You have a beautiful home," he murmured before turning to her. "And thanks for helping me put names and faces together. It's good for an investigation like this."

"Of course."

His glance went to the painting over the piano.

"I covet that oil of Mt. Timpanogos. The first time I drove south of Salt Lake, I saw it as I rounded a curve in the road. It's spectacular with snow on it."

"I think so, too. It's a painting my grandfather did years ago. He hiked that mountain many times when he was younger."

"I've meant to do it myself. One of these days I will."

"Won't you sit down?" She'd motioned to one of her striped Italian provincial chairs, noticing details about him as he took a seat. He wore his dark-blond hair fairly short. In the lamp light she glimpsed gold highlights on the tips, and the slight cleft in his chin. The rest of his features were hard, rugged male.

"I have a couple of questions," he began. "First, what should I wear to work in the morning?"

"Anything casual. Everyone who works there wears jeans. You'll be supplied an apron that goes around the neck."

"That sounds fine as long as my colleagues don't see me in it."

Mitch Garrett didn't need to worry. With his masculine features and tall, strong physique, he couldn't have been more manly. When Bruno had asked her to report to the Lufka P.I. firm, she'd pictured working with some overweight, middle-aged television-attorney type.

The midthirties man with brown eyes almost piercing in their intensity had come as a total surprise. Coupled with his dangerous, unconscious air of power, his image had refused to leave her mind and was now indelibly inscribed.

She flashed him a smile. "We make the donuts at

the back of the shop, so if any of your coworkers pop in when it opens, they won't see you."

"That relieves my mind more than you know. Now for the next question. What would be the best way for me to access your company's personnel files without going to your office? I need to see everything."

"If you'd like, after we've finished work tomorrow, we'll drive to your office and I'll download the files to your computer from my phone."

"Excellent. When will we be finished work?"

"By 9:00 a.m."

"Good. That means we'll have enough time to go over the names and backgrounds of the employees until you have to pick up your son. I'm going to need other kinds of information, too." He pulled a folded sheet of paper from his pocket and handed it to her. "If you can be prepared to answer these questions I've written here, our work will go faster."

"I'll go over them before I get in bed."

"You've been more than helpful already," he said, and before she was ready to see him go, he got to his feet. "I know six o'clock will come early, so I'll say good-night and we'll discuss everything else tomorrow."

Heidi walked him to the door. After he'd driven away, she sank down on the couch to read over his checklist. He wanted to know where every stop was along every route. He was so thorough, it was positively scary. Finally she got ready for bed, but it took her a long time to fall asleep. Today had turned into such a challenging day. A threat to the company from within the family ranks had prompted Bruno to hire a private investigator.

Of all the P.I.s out there, the man she'd been thrown into the middle of an investigation with was cast from a different mold than most men. If Jonas and Lucas were behind the thefts, they had no idea of the kind of force they were up against.

AFTER A SHOWER AND SHAVE, Mitch dressed in jeans and a T-shirt before leaving for the donut shop. When he pulled up in front of SweetSpuds, the sun had just peeked over Mount Olympus.

So many times he'd dropped by here on his way to work, never dreaming that one day he'd be making donuts with the most appealing woman he'd ever met. She seemed to have an inner beauty that made her whole being light up. By the end of the day today, he hoped he hadn't been imagining it. Too many times he'd been disappointed by some feeling he'd thought was real, only to discover otherwise. Over the past few years these letdowns had taken their toll, making him feel older than his years.

He got out of his car, noticing the sign on the glass door. Open eight to six, Monday through Saturday. Closed Sunday.

"Good morning, Mr. Garrett." She'd pulled in and parked next to him. When she climbed out of her Nissan, the sun gilded her mass of curls. His shuttered gaze took in the rest of her down to her sneakers. Yesterday she'd worn a suit. Today she was in jeans and a loose-fitting navy T-shirt. No matter what she wore, nothing could hide her gorgeous figure.

"Call me Mitch, please. Mind if I call you Heidi?"

"Not at all," she said, looking for the right key to open the shop door. He followed her inside. It was a small facility. Behind the counter he saw a door that led to the back room. Next to it were the tall racks of shelving that held the donuts. The place served coffee and soft drinks from the side counter. In the front were four small round tables and enough chairs to serve sixteen people at a time.

"Come through this door and we'll get started. The restroom for employees is back here, too."

The modern kitchen was outfitted with a massive fridge and all the necessary equipment, including a washer and dryer. Built-in shelves held the fifty-pound bags of mix with the blue tags. More shelves on wheels contained the donut trays. A half-dozen donuts remained in one of them. When she saw where his eyes had wandered, she said, "Help yourself, Mitch."

"Don't mind if I do." He reached for one with chocolate icing. "My boss told me I was going to love this job."

She chuckled. "Working here has ruined many a figure. I can't tell you the number of diets I've had to go on over the years." She handed him an apron from the cupboard, then grabbed one for herself.

As they put them on, Mitch flicked her another glance. He decided not to comment that her efforts obviously hadn't been in vain. There wasn't an ounce of surplus flesh he could see on her anywhere. "Did you always work for the company?"

"Yes," she replied. "My parents' home isn't far from here. Dad started me off in this shop when I was old enough to sweep floors and help do cleanup. I was probably nine. Slowly I graduated to more duties.

"By high school I was making donuts and selling them after school and on Saturdays. I put myself through college in this shop. Later on I worked in the plant learning every job, then I was transferred to headquarters where I've been in charge of payroll and now personnel."

"Sounds like you've done it all. Will you start Zack out here when he's nine?"

"I don't know yet. He's got a mind of his own."

"Meaning you didn't?" he teased.

"My dad was my idol and still is. I'd do anything for him." Her gaze met his. "Do you feel that way about yours?"

"I never knew my parents," he said. "I was a baby abandoned in a church in Tallahassee, Florida. Someone found me lying inside an orange crate with the words Garrett Fruit Company stamped on it. I was always called the Garrett boy."

Heidi let out a quiet cry.

"When I got old enough I called myself Mitch. I don't know why. It's one of those stories you read about on occasion and can't believe. I went from foster home to foster home. At eighteen I joined the Marines. Don't get me wrong. It's been a good life, but a different one. It wasn't my destiny to have a family of my own."

She didn't move a muscle, but her eyes darkened with emotion. "I'm sorry to have asked you that question. My home life was pretty idyllic. For a minute I forgot that not everyone starts out the same way."

"There's no need to apologize, Heidi. Most people know their parents, or know of them. I'd have given anything to know either parent. I don't have a clue about my heritage on either side. If I have siblings or relatives, I'm not aware of them. No connections of any kind make me think your Zack is the luckiest of boys to have come from a family like yours you can date back to the nineteenth century."

"I...I think he is, too." Her voice caught, then she cleared her throat. "If you'll wash your hands, I'll give you some gloves to put on and we'll get started." He watched her put on a hairnet before joining him at the sink. Her little blue earrings glinted through the netting. No matter what she did, she exuded a sensuality he doubted she was even aware of. But Mitch was feeling it and had to fight hard to concentrate on the task at hand.

Once the vat of oil was heating, she measured the mix from the bag and put it in the hopper, adding the precise amount of liquid ingredients. After the batter was power-mixed, she checked the oil to be sure it was the right temperature. Then she turned the switch and the dough dropped down through nozzles into the fat. He watched in fascination as rotors turned the donuts over at proper intervals and then moved them onto a conveyor belt for a sugar glaze. Soon they were guided onto trays.

"This goes fast because we use baking powder rather than yeast," she explained. Before he knew it, she'd done another batch. This time it went through a chocolate-glazing process. Another batch received a white glaze with multicolored sprinkles, another with nuts. Already an hour had gone by. "Our general rule of thumb is to make sixteen hundred donuts a day."

"That's a lot of donuts."

"I know, but the high school and college students will eat up a thousand of them by two in the afternoon. Would you believe we usually run out ten minutes before closing?"

"Yup. I've come here at the last minute and had to go away hungry."

Her laugh delighted him. "Okay, we've already made eight hundred. Now let's see you mix the next batch of dough in the hopper."

He did all right, but she had to caution him to check the heat on the oil again. "The frying oil is the most expensive ingredient in the production process, and if the donuts absorb too much oil, it reduces the profit margin."

You learned something new every day, Mitch thought. Somehow he managed to cook the second eight hundred without the place going up in flames.

She grinned when he let out a sigh of relief. "I know how you feel. Good job! Now comes the part we all hate."

"The cleanup," he muttered as he put the last of the loaded trays on the shelves.

"You catch on fast. I'll wheel out this stack of trays to the front. It's eight o'clock. Phyllis should be here by now setting up."

They worked like a team washing the equipment, making everything so spick and span the kitchen gleamed. The vat of oil was cooled and discarded in metal containers she placed outside the rear door. After she removed her hairnet, they took off their gloves and aprons and did a wash that included towels and cloths. While they waited for everything to dry, he mopped the floor.

She eyed him over her shoulder. "You don't have

to do that. We have a janitorial service that comes in every night."

"After doing KP duty, I'm afraid it's a habit. Tell me something. How many of these shops do you own around the Valley?"

"Twenty."

"I imagine their inventory is all sold out by the end of the day, too."

"Always."

"I've noticed that donuts get a bad rap by the media."

"Our company is a great target for the people screaming about obesity, but the sales don't change. Self-control is everyone's problem, not the fault of the free enterprise system."

He smiled at her. "My sentiments exactly." Mitch liked the way she thought. In fact, there wasn't anything about her he didn't like, and that feeling was growing stronger by the second.

As he put the mop away in the utility closet she asked, "How long have you been a P.I.?"

Mitch had been waiting for that question to come up. He shut the door and turned to her. "Ten months or so."

Judging by the silence, his answer had surprised her. "Then you're barely out of the Marines."

"Not exactly." He took a steadying breath. "Tell you what. Before we go to my office, let's head to the Cowboy Grub for breakfast and I'll answer your questions. Have you ever eaten there?"

She finished folding everything from the dryer and put things away. "Many times. It's close to the office and one of my favorite places."

"And mine. I'm glad we're in agreement because I'm starving. Sugar does that to me. I should never have eaten a donut on an empty stomach."

"I'm afraid I learned the same lesson a long time ago." She started out the self-locking rear door ahead of him.

It was ten after nine and already there were half a dozen cars, not counting theirs and Phyllis's, in the parking area. He got a sense of satisfaction from realizing those people would be eating the donuts he and Heidi had cooked from scratch. They weren't just any donuts. That recipe had come from the Old World, guarded and unchanged to this day.

As he helped her into her car, their glances met briefly. He felt the strangest sensation lift the hairs on the back of his neck. The culprits had been emboldened enough to have stolen hundreds of bags of mix, maybe more by now. If they suspected someone was on to them, they could present a physical danger to those around them. He didn't like the idea of her being anywhere near.

Chapter Three

Heidi sat in a booth across from Mitch. He'd ordered cinnamon rolls with his eggs and bacon. She'd decided on a ham omelet and corn bread. As she munched on the last of it, she said, "I won't need to eat another thing until tomorrow. If you want to know a secret, I've tried to figure out this restaurant's recipe for their bread since the first time I tasted it."

He eyed her steadily over the rim of his coffee cup. "You still don't have it down pat and refined?"

"Afraid not."

"Are you as big a whiz in the kitchen as you are making donuts at the shop?"

"I love to cook, but when you have a little boy who doesn't eat a lot and prefers a peanut butter and honey sandwich to anything else, there's not much point. What about you? Do you turn into a master chef when you go home to your family at night?" Since they were working together, she would at least like to know his marital status. If he had a wife, the knowledge might help her to stop the fantasizing.

After draining his coffee, he put the cup down, submitting her to a frank regard. "I never married and am better at warming up a frozen TV dinner."

Never married? It went to show that she really didn't have a clue about men. Furthermore, a whole history of unknowns lay behind his smile, but there was one thing she did know for certain. He was the most exciting man she'd ever met.

"I'm surprised," she responded and wiped the corner of her mouth with a napkin. "When we were talking about my son's haircut, you sounded so knowledgeable, I got the impression you must have children."

"No, but I do know a lot about little orphan boys who need to act tough and are counting the hours until they're free to make their own choices."

Heidi couldn't comprehend his life, but it wasn't difficult to imagine how hard it would have been trying to fit into a foster family. He'd said he'd had more than one. "Did you always want to go into the military?"

"No, but after high school it seemed to be one of the fastest ways to get an education funded. I put the time into pay back Uncle Sam's loan, then got out and went to work as a federal marshal. I've been one for six years."

Federal marshal.

They live dangerous lives.

"Meaning you still are?" Everything he told her came as a surprise, intriguing her. She realized he'd had a harder fight from the beginning than most people. And it had turned him into the kind of man she and her great-uncle wanted on their side.

"I'm on medical leave. I was shot in the shoulder and flown out here to TOSH for the surgery and rehab."

She winced. "Shot?"

"To make a long story short, an escaped felon who wanted revenge tried to kill the judge who'd sent him to prison. I was on duty to protect him. In the process of saving the Honorable Judge Wilken, I had to kill the felon. But I hadn't counted on him having another prison escapee for a partner named Whitey Filmore. We exchanged gunfire and I got the worst of it."

"What happened to him?"

"He's still on the loose."

Her stomach clenched. "That's terrifying."

"It's the nature of the business I'm in. Recently there's been a dramatic increase in the number of threats against members of the judiciary. Our department assesses the level of danger. On average, about a hundred threats are logged each year. We develop a plan to determine the appropriate preventive response for each one."

"In other words you always have to watch your back," she said, tight-lipped.

"Yes, but I didn't do such a good job that time. During the recovery period after the surgery, my boss contacted Roman Lufka, the owner you met at the P.I. firm, and he put me to work so I wouldn't go crazy with nothing to do."

"You mean your boss got you out of the way to preserve your life."

"That, too." His smile didn't make her feel relieved or reassured. "I've received expert medical care and I'm now fully recovered."

She didn't realize she'd been holding her breath. "That's a great blessing. Your health is everything."

"Agreed. Once I've solved your case, in all likelihood I'll be going back to Tallahassee."

The news that he'd be returning to Florida shouldn't matter to her, but to know what awaited him made her sick inside. She bit her lip. "If you go back, he'll be lying in wait for you."

"That's a chance I'll have to take. Somebody has to do the job. We can't allow our judges to be killed off because there's no protection for them. Where would our country be if we didn't have men and women fighting for our freedoms?"

"You're right, of course." But she didn't have to like it. "Do you miss Tallahassee?"

"Not particularly, but it's where I was found and grew up. When I was in the group home, I used to think my birth mother might come looking for me if I stayed put."

His words pained Heidi. She averted her eyes. "Did you try looking for her?"

"I went through that stage, but as I grew older, I realized she might not have been Floridian and was only looking for the nearest church to leave her baby on her way to somewhere else. I went through every conceivable Garrett name asking questions, but received no satisfactory answers. It seemed a hopeless quest.

"By then I'd decided to go into the military. Occasionally I still write to the Bureau of Vital Statistics in Tallahassee to search for any new Garrett names that I can check out. In fact, just yesterday I received a letter suggesting I contact a genealogist."

"Bruno's the big genealogist in our family. If you asked him, I'm sure he'd have contacts who could help you."

"I might do that."

"What other sources have you investigated?"

"I've left my name and phone number with the church where I was found and the group home, even with my foster parents, in case someone inquires about me."

Heidi feared she was going to break down and have a huge cry. "Don't ever give up, Mitch. One day maybe a miracle will happen."

"Maybe." He didn't sound hopeful. "Even if I did find either of my parents, they obviously don't want to be found. I'm not sure it would change anything except to satisfy my curiosity over what kind of people they are or what they look like. It's probably better I don't find them."

But he wants to. Heidi took a quick breath. "You've led an extraordinary life. We have a Marine in my great-aunt Barbara's family. Rob says it was an experience he wouldn't have missed for the world."

"He's right."

Their conversation had left her drained. She was ready to leave. "Thank you for breakfast, Mitch. It was delicious."

"You're welcome."

"I'm ready to leave for your office and download the files whenever you're ready," she said. "I know my great-uncle Bruno is anxious to put an end to the stealing and is grateful for your firm's help."

"I'm grateful for the work."

Mitch sounded sincere, but being a P.I. couldn't compare to his chosen career as a federal marshal. He pulled out his wallet and put enough money on the table to cover their bill. "Let's go."

They both got to their feet and headed for the door of the restaurant. One of the waitresses smiled at him. She'd probably waited on him before. Throughout their meal Heidi had noticed several females staring at him in unabashed admiration. She'd struggled not to do the same.

Once in their cars, she followed him to his office and parked alongside him. After she got out, he called to her. He was leaning across the seat and had opened the passenger door.

"Before we get started on those files, I've decided I'd like to drive out to Woods Cross with you in order to get a visual of the plant facility. We can go in my car and return within the hour. Do you have sunglasses?"

"Yes."

"Good. To be sure no one recognizes you, I'll run inside our shop and find something to cover those curls. Be right back."

Heidi climbed into his Audi and drew her glasses case from her bag. Pretty soon he'd returned with a straw gardening hat that tied under the chin. She put it on with her sunglasses.

"I can't believe you found anything so perfect."

"The P.I. business often calls for a disguise. We keep all kinds of things on hand for emergencies. This early in the investigation we can't afford for you to be recognized while I'm looking around."

"I'm so covered up, no one will know who I am." Heidi loved the idea.

He started up his car and they headed north. "I've only driven past Woods Cross on my way to Ogden on business. Tell me about it."

She peered at his arresting profile through her sunglasses. "Do you want the family reunion version that goes on and on? We have one every year and the tales get longer." He chuckled. "Or, I can give you information on a need-to-know basis."

He maneuvered expertly through the morning traffic. "I want to hear what Heidi Bauer Norris would like me to know if I were a tourist out here visiting for the first time."

"Once I get started, you might be sorry—tell me if you get bored. Okay, let's see. Woods Cross lies near the bottom of the Great Salt Lake Basin and is located eight miles north of Salt Lake.

"The town of nine thousand was officially chartered in 1935, but was originally a big unincorporated area with the Great Salt Lake on one side and the mountains on the other. Saska's family of ten emigrated here in 1892. Her parents and grandmother were ailing and she had six siblings to feed. With the little money they'd pooled, she rented a shack and immediately planted potatoes. With the sales from her sweet buns, she bought up land bit by bit, and their first plant was erected on it.

"It was hard work because they had to build wooden troughs and ditches along the watersheds of the foothills to channel the water where they wanted it to go. Saska herself helped install drains to carry the excess to the Great Salt Lake. Her family also built holding ponds and an underground cistern to save the runoff.

"Today I'll show you the place in the foothills where we have a ranch house and horses. On the site is the original shack and plant. Below it is the modern facility. You'll notice the fleet of trucks and garage for the mechanics farther on.

"My relatives Sylvia and her husband Daniel Bauer live on the ranch year round with their five children to maintain it. Zack and I come out here riding every chance we get. My dad joins us when he can. Right now they're building a float for the Days of '47 parade coming up on the twenty-fourth."

"I've heard about it, but I wasn't flown here until last August and missed it."

"It's our state holiday commemorating the arrival of the pioneers in the Salt Lake Valley in 1847. The parade is next Monday. Maybe you'll have time to see it."

"I'll *make* time for it."

He was getting to her more and more. She took a deep breath and went on, "This year the children will be wearing pioneer clothes and riding on the float. Zack can't wait. Daniel will be driving the float behind my father, who'll be riding his horse. He's the grand marshal. The parade committee asked him to open the parade this year."

Mitch turned his head toward her. "A marshal, you say?"

"Yeah. How about that. In a cowboy hat, no less."

This time he flashed her a broad smile. You wouldn't think it could affect her so, but what else would have made her heart suddenly double thump in reaction?

The man was a quick study. Inside of twenty minutes he'd seen what was needed by driving around the plant while she answered his questions. On their way back to Salt Lake, he pulled into a popular Mexican restaurant. "I'm hungry," he declared. "If you're not, please humor me. I've been dreaming of their fish tacos wrapped in blue tortillas since early morning."

A soft laugh escaped her lips. "I love them, too. For your information, I'm starving." She removed the gardening hat he'd given her.

"You're a woman after my own heart." For a second she had the feeling he wanted to kiss her. For much longer than that, she'd wanted him to. It was insane. Crazy.

After they'd gone inside and ordered, the waitress brought them virgin margaritas. "Have you always loved Mexican food?" She couldn't learn enough about him.

"If it's good, yeah."

"My thoughts exactly."

He flashed her a sly look. "How come you always agree with me?"

An imp got into her. "You're the P.I. Let me know when you've figured it out."

His deep laughter resonated inside her.

BEFORE LONG THEY RETURNED to Mitch's office. "That was well worth the time," he said as she sat down in the chair opposite his desk. "I can now picture the single-story layout from one end of the plant to the other." But the picture he preferred was the one of Heidi seated across his desk.

She'd brought the gardening hat in from the car and laid it on his desk. Her hair was a golden mass he wanted to plunder. "Better yet, no one knew I was there."

Except for Mitch, who would have kidnapped her

if he'd thought he could get away with it. "The ranch in those green foothills is a wonderful spread."

"As I think I told you, Zack and I love to go riding there." She pulled out her iPhone to start the download.

"I can understand why. Saska chose the perfect spot to settle. When you see the growth of the communities north of Salt Lake, it makes you appreciate your ancestor's vision in buying the land before others discovered the value of the area."

"In her diary she mentioned how many times someone came along trying to get her to sell, but they didn't know her." Heidi's voice rang with pride. "Saska had a dream."

"One that your great-uncle Bruno is determined to keep alive. More than ever I'm anxious to catch the persons responsible," he asserted. "To get started, why don't you draw me an organizational chart showing the heads of the different divisions and who reports to whom. I'll read over the pertinent information from their files and you can fill me in on anything else you know that might be significant."

They worked for several hours. Mitch found her an unending source of knowledge. Between that and her sunny disposition, he enjoyed every minute with her. After studying the files complete with ID photos, he said, "While we've been going over the information on everyone who works there now, I've made a list of the names of those people who've left the company in the last five years.

"I need to know why they left. Was it for maternity leave? A higher-paying job? Or maybe a move out of the city or state? Are they still friendly with any of the workers who are there now? Do any of them have a grudge you're aware of? Maybe some who are disgruntled? Anything you can tell me will help."

She nodded and they dug into working through that list. Eventually he made up another list consisting of ten nonfamily workers let go by the company. According to Heidi, they'd been fired for every reason—from being habitually late to calling in sick too many times to being sloppy on the job. One of the truck drivers had complained that they didn't pay him enough money for the work he did and he didn't finish a delivery to Arizona.

"What about this last name, Gary Norris? Any connection?" He flicked his gaze to her.

"He's my ex-husband."

Mitch had assumed as much and studied the picture in the file. Nice-looking guy with brown hair and blue eyes. Born in Salem, Oregon. Attended University of Utah two semesters. Started out working at the counter part-time at the No. 2 shop at Bauer's seven years ago. Graduated to full-time as a baker and assistant manager. Two years later transferred to plant. Worked in the warehouse until terminated two years ago at the age of twenty-nine.

Already Mitch didn't like him. "Being that he was your spouse, it couldn't have been an easy decision to fire him. Who actually let him go?"

Heidi held his gaze. "My father. If you were to ask Dad why, he'd tell you it was Gary's attitude. Basically he wanted an upper-management position, but it's company policy to have obtained an MBA first in order to rise to the top. Bruno and Dad are adamant about that. They believe it shows a person has stuck to something long enough to understand the persistence it takes to run a company."

"College does that for you," he concurred. "When I was reading their backgrounds, I noticed that of those of your family still living, your aunt Marcia, you and your brother, Rich, are the only Bauers besides your father and great-uncle who obtained an MBA."

"Yes. I attended the U of U at night and worked during the day, but Gary didn't like school. He's not the only one. Four of my cousins work at the plant, yet none of them wants to study that hard even though the company has set up a fund to pay half tuition for anyone wanting to go to college."

"Lucky people who decide to take advantage of it. What does your ex-husband do now?"

"I have no idea. After he was fired, I divorced him for personal reasons. He's gone back to Oregon where he was born and raised."

"Then how do the two of you work out visitation with your son?"

She looked away. "We don't. He couldn't get out of the marriage and fatherhood fast enough."

Mitch couldn't comprehend a man doing that. To have a wife and son, then turn his back on both of them, especially on a woman like Heidi.... It was anathema to him.

Your birth father apparently did the same to you, Garrett.

Odd how the two situations didn't seem comparable.

"Forgive me for asking that question, Heidi. It's none of my business."

"There's nothing to forgive," she murmured. "The

truth is, while we were dating, Gary told me how much he looked forward to being a father one day, but once Zack was born, he showed virtually no interest in him. After we divorced, he never paid child support."

"You didn't take him back to court?"

She shook her head. "You have to understand something. I make a good enough income on my own and always have. He was counting on that. Throughout our marriage and more so by the end of it, he accused me of being born with a silver spoon in my mouth.

"I simply didn't know how to fight his flawed logic. Everyone in our family works hard. There are no shortcuts to success. Before he packed his bags, Gary told me that living around us was like wearing a straitjacket." She paused. "Have I shocked you?"

Mitch sat forward. "How could I be shocked when I grew up not even knowing who my father was? But I'll admit I'm saddened for your son's sake by what you've told me."

"Toward the end of our failed marriage, I cried my eyes out for Zack's sake. But I got over it when my attorney informed me Gary had given up his parental rights and had signed papers to that effect. By that time nothing really surprised me, because by then I realized what my dad had said was true. Every man can make a baby, but that doesn't necessarily make him a parent."

"Amen," Mitch said. "Evidently my parents came to that realization the moment I was born. Does your son know his father gave up all claims to him?"

"Not yet. I'm waiting for the proper time to tell him, but I'm not sure when that will be."

Before they traveled down that path any further, he

quickly changed the subject and turned to the computer once more. "I see here that Jonas Bauer attended Westminster College in Salt Lake for two years, but didn't finish."

She nodded. "If you study the applications carefully, you'll find that forty percent of the employees, family or not, have some credits beyond high school, but not enough to move higher. The rest either started with the company after graduation from high school, or worked at different jobs before coming to Bauer's."

The more he learned, the more Mitch imagined this highly successful, family-owned company was like one of those old pressure cookers that built up steam. Without a release valve, you could count on some kind of explosion. Mitch was eager to get inside the plant and find out who was doing what.

He saw her glance at her watch, reminding him it was getting late. "We've accomplished a lot today, Heidi, but I can see it's time to let you go so you can pick up Zack. Thanks for working with me all day. This is a great beginning."

Much as he didn't want her to leave, he had no choice but to get up from his chair and walk her out to her car. "I'll see you at six tomorrow morning."

After she slid in behind the wheel, she flicked him a wicked glance. In full sunlight, her eyes and hair gleamed, dazzling him. "Thanks for the delicious lunch. For a reward, tomorrow I'll let you make all the donuts." He chuckled. "If you pass the test, then you'll be ready to move on to greater things."

Greater things meant no more just the two of them.

Mitch could wish this part of the training period lasted longer. Heidi was growing on him in quantum leaps. Instead of needing his own space, he found he wanted her to share it with him. He was disappointed, in fact, that he had to wait until tomorrow to see her again.

Their conversation had touched as much on the personal as on the thefts that had brought her to the P.I. firm. He rarely opened up to anyone, but to her he had, and she'd put her finger on the truth about one thing— Lew had two motives for sending Mitch to Utah; the first that he would receive the best medical care, the second that he'd be kept out of harm's way for a time.

Long enough for him to have met Heidi Norris.

After seeing her off, he went back to work, checking backgrounds on the ten nonfamily members let go from the company in the past five years. Each would have worked with Jonas and his son.

Of the ten on the list, only one had been a woman. Her job had been to work in the mix division. Of the nine men, eight of them had worked in the warehouse. The other one was the truck driver Heidi had told him about. Only two of the men, Dennis Blake and Gary Norris, had been fired within three weeks of each other and might have become friends in their mutual dissatisfaction with the rules.

Mitch found he couldn't get his mind off Heidi's ex-husband. His leaving her and their son without any concern for their welfare was incredibly selfish. Mitch had known a few guys in the military who'd abandoned their wives and children, but now that he'd met Heidi, he couldn't fathom how any man could give her up.

With a grimace, he purposely returned his mind to the task at hand. The employees on the list who'd left the Bauer company needed to be investigated. He was curious to see what they were doing with their lives now. It was a painstaking process, but once Mitch was working inside the plant, he'd pick up information fast.

"ZACK? BREAKFAST IS READY." Heidi had made scrambled eggs and toast.

Her son came in the kitchen dragging his backpack. "I don't want to go to Aunt Sharon's."

She finished pouring his orange juice. "How come?"

"Cuz I want to be with you."

"You can't, honey. I'm training a pri—a new employee this morning." She'd almost let it slip. Zack knew about private investigators after watching all the super-sleuth shows on the cartoon network. If her boy caught wind of who Mitch really was, he'd tell his cousin, and soon Sharon and Rich would know about it. Then the questions would start and word could leak out to the company, destroying Bruno's plan to catch whoever was stealing unawares.

"But I don't want them to drive me to school."

Heidi sat down to eat with him, but so far he hadn't touched his food. "Why not?"

"Because Uncle Rich is going to take us. He wants to talk to Jenny's teacher."

Something was wrong here. "Why do you care?"

"He's not my dad."

"He loves you, Zack."

His blue eyes filled with tears. "I don't want to go to school with them." He took off for his bedroom. Heidi raced after him and nearly collided with the door he was trying to shut.

"Honey…" She picked him up and held him close while he cried. "I've never seen you act like this before. Did your uncle hurt your feelings?"

"No."

"Did Tim?"

"No."

"Then help me understand." She lowered him to the floor, then sat on the end of his twin bed so they could talk.

He refused to look at her. "The other kids know he's not my dad."

She was trying hard to figure this out. "Why does that matter?"

More tears rolled down his flushed cheeks. "They'll ask me where my dad is."

A pain stabbed her heart. "Oh. I see." She *did* see and this situation wasn't going to be resolved with one conversation. Heidi wondered how long Zack had been actively dealing with this burden. Weeks? Months? The problem was, she'd run out of time. Mitch was probably at the shop right now waiting to be let in. The conversation they needed would have to wait.

"Tell you what, honey. Come to work with me, and I'll drive you to school at eight, but you'll have to sit at one of the tables and read while I'm training this person."

His face brightened. "Okay."

"Come on. Let's hurry out to the car. Grab the toast I made for you."

While he did her bidding, she reached for his back-pack and they dashed through the connecting door to the garage. En route to the shop, Heidi phoned her brother. She thanked him and Sharon for being willing to help out, then told him there'd been a change in plans.

Sure enough, Mitch's Audi sat in the empty parking lot. When she pulled up next to him, he levered himself from the driver's seat, looking incredibly attractive in a yellow polo shirt and jeans that molded to his powerful thighs.

After Zack got out of the backseat, he was all eyes.

She reached for the backpack on the front seat. "Zack, I'd like you to meet Mitch Garrett, who's in training for our company. Mitch, this is my son, Zack."

"Hi, Zack." Mitch got down on his haunches in front of him, giving him his full attention.

"Hi." Zack spoke right up.

"I like your haircut. When I was in the Marines, we all had to wear one like yours. It feels good on a hot day."

"Yeah." Her boy grinned. "How long were you in the Marines?"

"Ten years."

"Wow." Zack paused for a moment, then said, "Did you have to do a lot of...well, you know...scary stuff?"

Mitch nodded.

"Do you ever get nightmares?" Zack's question astonished Heidi.

"Sometimes. How about you?"

"Sometimes after I've played a zombie video game at my cousin's house. My aunt doesn't know Tim traded one of his Indiana Jones Lego games for it." Heidi didn't know that. No wonder he sometimes cried out in the night and got into her bed.

"I've played that game before, but those zombies are harmless."

"I know," Zack said, "but they're different in my dreams."

Mitch smiled. "Next time they're in your dreams, knock them over with one of those golf carts or the lawn mower."

"Yeah."

"The thing is, they're not real. That's why they're pathetic. Do you notice how they walk slow and wobble?"

"Especially that old man," Zack pointed out.

"Yeah. The one with the hat pulled over one eye."

While both of them were laughing about the game, relating perfectly, Heidi stood there in mild shock. Zack was normally a boy of few words except with family. Hearing him now, she saw a different child from the one she'd been raising for six years. Mitch was wonderful with him, trying to help him not be afraid.

"Do you live around here?" Zack asked him.

"Let me ask *you* a question. Do you ever go to the Hogle Zoo?"

"Yeah. I go with my mom a lot."

"Well, I live in an apartment near the street that takes you up there."

She could hear her son's mind working. "Hey, Mom—"

"Zack—" she broke in, having a hunch where this conversation could be headed "—Mitch and I have work to do making donuts." Heidi opened the door of the shop and they filed in. "I want you to find a table and get out your homework. You're falling behind on your summer reading program."

"Okay. Can I come and watch in a few minutes?"

"Yes, but you'll have to be quiet. Mitch has to concentrate."

"Yeah," the P.I. agreed, regarding Heidi with a devilish gleam in his eye. "It's a lot harder than peeling potatoes."

He would have been good at that, she thought. She realized he was good at everything, including talking to children.

"Hey, Mitch," Zack said, "did you know our donuts are made from potatoes?"

"That's what your mother told me. You know what I think?"

"What?" Her son was mesmerized by this man.

"There ought to be a cartoon like SpongeBob called SweetSpud."

"Yeah!" Zack exclaimed. "That would be so cool!"

"Okay, Zack, no more talking." Heidi undid his backpack and pulled out two of the books he was supposed to read. "I'll come and check on you in a little while."

"I want some of Mitch's donuts when they're done."

"I'll bring one home for you after school. No donuts without a good lunch first."

Chapter Four

Mitch washed his hands and got into his garb before he started mixing the dough. "That's quite a little guy you've got there. Smart and funny."

"I've never seen him that open with a stranger before."

"Video games are the universal language with kids, young or old."

She laughed. "Being a Marine didn't hurt, either."

"It's a credit to you that he's an all-American boy. Now that I've met him, I have to tell you again you're a lucky mom." Mitch warmed up the oil and started cooking while she watched his movements. He was a fast learner. She didn't have to remind him of anything.

"You're right. I love him to death, but I need to apologize for bringing him to work with me this morning. He wanted to be with me and wouldn't let my brother drive him to school. I'll have to leave here at eight to take him. But I won't be gone more than ten minutes. You can enjoy a break."

"If I'd had a mom, I would have wanted to be with her, too."

Halfway through the second batch of eight hundred

her son walked in the kitchen. He moved over by Heidi and watched Mitch making donuts.

"Hi, sport."

Zack beamed. "Hi! Is that fun?"

Those midnight-brown eyes glanced at him with affection. "It sure is. When you're a little older, you'll be able to make them, too."

"I know."

"Have you finished your homework?"

"No." He sighed. "I needed a break."

Laughter rumbled out of Mitch. "What are you reading for school?"

"Dumb stories."

"That's no fun. What do you like to read?"

"Spy stories."

"So do I. What are your favorites?"

"*The Black Paw* and *Spectacular Spy Capers.*"

Heidi heard the surprise in Mitch's voice as he said, "You're talking the Spy Mice?"

"Yeah!"

"Now *those* are fun!"

"Mom—" Zack looked up at Heidi "—Mitch likes them, too."

"Isn't that amazing?" She exchanged amused glances with Mitch before the last of the dough dropped from the nozzles into the oil. The donuts cooked for the exact amount of time before he put them through the glaze. "Your performance was excellent, Mr. Garrett. You get A plus."

"That's a gross exaggeration, but I'm glad it met with your approval."

"You're on track to be moved to the plant."

While she tried without success to tear her gaze

from his, Zack said, "I'm going to be a spy when I grow up."

Mitch's warm smile settled on her son. "Guess what? I have a friend who owns a spy shop with all kinds of stuff."

His blue eyes rounded. "Could I see it?"

"I guess that depends on your mom. Maybe both of you would like to come."

"Mom!" This time Zack's cry of delight reverberated off the kitchen walls. "Can we go after school? Please?"

Mitch's invitation was perfectly natural, considering the direction of the conversation with Zack. But if she accepted, it put their relationship on a different footing. She'd be crossing that line from the professional to the personal. After her disastrous marriage, she'd been guarding herself against making another bad decision where a man was concerned. Besides, Mitch would be going back to Florida after he'd discovered who was stealing their donut mix.

"Honey, we don't even know if Mitch will be available this afternoon."

Mitch had removed his apron. "I'll be free to meet you there, but you might have other plans. Why don't you two talk about it on the way to school and let me know?"

School— That's right. It was eight o'clock. Heidi was supposed to be driving him right now. Instead, her head had been somewhere else...concentrating on someone else.

She quickly took off her apron and gloves. "Come on, Zack. We'll be late if we don't leave now."

"Okay," he said in a grumpy voice. "But I wish I didn't have to go to school. See you later, Mitch."

"See you, sport."

Heidi hustled him out of the kitchen. He pulled his backpack off the table. They met the shop manager coming in the front door.

"Hi, Phyllis," said Heidi. "Mr. Garrett's in back starting to clean up. I won't be long. I've got to run Zack to school."

As Zack headed for the car, Phyllis said, "I caught a glimpse of Mr. Gorgeous yesterday. What a hunk!" Phyllis was happily married with three older children, but she still had eyes to see.

"He didn't make a mistake with the donuts, either. Will Jim be here tomorrow?"

"That's what his wife told me last night."

"Let me know if there's a problem."

"Will do."

Heidi hurried out to the car. During the drive, all Zack talked about was Mitch. By the time they reached the school, where the children were lined up to go inside, she couldn't take any more of his pleading.

"If it's still all right with Mitch, we'll stop by his friend's shop for a few minutes after school, but you have to remember he's a busy man."

"I will." To her shock, he undid the strap of his car seat and leaned forward to give her a kiss on the cheek before climbing out of the car. He was so excited, he forgot to act like a big guy.

When she got back to the shop and helped with the rest of the cleanup, she told Mitch he'd made her son's day.

"Do you want to know something?" He'd just pulled

the items out of the dryer to fold and put away. His gaze darted to hers. "You've just made mine by telling me you'll bring him to the office after school."

The way he was looking at her produced a fluttery sensation in her chest. "Just keep in mind he's at a very impressionable age and will drive you crazy with questions."

"He's wonderful. What time do you think you'll be there?"

"Around twenty to four."

"I'm headed there now to keep working on background checks. That's going to take hours. I'll meet you in the parking lot and we'll go into the shop directly. He'll never know the attached office is my place of business."

She nodded. "I'm interested in seeing it myself."

"Roman's brother manufactures spy equipment back east and ships it to him. When Zack gets in there, he's never going to want to leave, so be warned." The warning bells were already going off for Heidi, but already she'd ignored them by agreeing to meet him over something that had nothing to do with the case.

A minute later they walked through to the front of the donut shop. As they went out the door to the parking lot, Phyllis winked at Heidi. This was how gossip got started. Thankfully today was Mitch's last day making donuts.

Before they parted company she said, "I'm going to run by Bruno's house and tell him what's going on. Now that you've had your crash course, it's time to move you to the warehouse where the bags are loaded onto the trucks. He'll arrange it with Randy, who's responsible for working out the shifts."

"I'd like to start work there on Friday because I have other plans for tomorrow. What's the schedule for the employees at the plant in terms of lunch?"

"Everyone takes the same one-hour break at twelve."

"Is there a lunchroom?"

"Yes. Some bring their food and eat in there. Others leave and go out for a bite."

"Ask your great-uncle to arrange for the fire department to have an evacuation of the building during the lunch hour tomorrow. That way the employees will be prepared. An evacuation means everyone out—no exceptions—while the fire department does a safety inspection to see if everything is in compliance since the last inspection. It'll give me time to plant some surveillance cameras and listening devices."

How incredibly clever.

"While I'm in there, I'll get a good look at the interior layout, including the offices for Jonas and Lucas. I want to see what they have on file and on the computer."

"What if they have a password Bruno doesn't know?"

"No problem. If it becomes necessary, our firm has the technology to get into the hard drive."

Obviously nothing was impossible for Mitch. She'd heard the FBI had the means to crack millions of passwords per second.

"Today while we're in Roman's shop, I'll pick out the equipment I need. Zack can help me without knowing what I'm doing."

Mitch's brilliant mind never stopped working. "He'll be in heaven."

"What do you say we go for a pizza afterward? We should all be hungry by then. The Pizza Oven is practically next door. We can walk to it."

Her toe was already in the water. Why not go all the way and plunge in, just this once? "We'd love it. Now I don't have to worry about what to fix for dinner."

"And it saves me from having to eat frozen fish sticks."

She smiled before they parted company. Heidi took off for Bruno's two-story Cape Cod house on upper Yalecrest, not that far from the apartment where Mitch lived. To think he'd been in Salt Lake for the past year, but she'd had no knowledge of him until Monday afternoon….

Bruno's eyes gleamed when she told him Mitch's plan. He got right on his part of it and gave her the go-ahead for the P.I. to do whatever he wanted. Heidi drove back to her house and did some laundry before it was time to pick up Zack.

He came flying out of the school to her car. It didn't take long to reach the Lufka firm.

"There's Mitch!"

Heidi had already spotted the hard-muscled man in the yellow polo and her heart began to thud without mercy. He was so handsome, she could croak. That's what her sister, Evy, would say if she ever saw him.

Zack scrambled out of the car. Mitch seemed to look at her with male pleasure before he greeted her son and walked them around the back of the private shop not open to the public. He unlocked the door and ushered them inside.

When he turned on the lights, she found herself looking at a treasure trove of gadgets and equipment.

Zack walked around inspecting everything, his eyes big as saucers. "Oh, man!" he blurted several times, obviously having picked up the expression from some kids at school. She heard Mitch's deep chuckle in the background.

"Oh, man" was right.

MITCH SAT IN THE BOOTH across from Heidi and Zack, enjoying the view. "More pizza anyone?"

Her blue eyes widened. "You're joking."

He chuckled. "I was just making sure."

"Zack never eats two whole pieces. I don't think he could find room for another bite."

"This pizza's good," Zack declared. "What's that meat called?"

"Canadian bacon," Mitch answered.

"Yum. I wish I could live in that spy shop. Then when I get hungry I could walk over here."

His comment was too much. Mitch's laughter merged with Heidi's. Her son was an entertaining, lovable little character with a huge imagination. He surmised Heidi had a full-time job on her hands keeping up with him.

"I'm glad you had fun in there."

"I loved it! Do you think your friend would let me look around again sometime?"

"Zack..."

"Whenever you'd like. Just ask your mom." Mitch reached for the sack at his side. "While we're still on the subject, I wanted you to have this."

Zack took it from him. "What is it?"

"Look inside."

The boy's hands were trembling as he pulled out a box, but it was fastened up tight.

"Here. Let me help you." Mitch undid everything. "These are walkie-talkies that fit on a bike. You can let a friend put one of these on his bike, and then when you go riding, you can talk to each other while you spy."

Mitch didn't know what he expected, but was surprised when Zack lowered his head and didn't say anything. "Hey…if you don't like these, I'll take them back and get you something else you'd rather have."

An anxious expression crossed Heidi's face. "He loves these, don't you, honey?"

Zack nodded.

"Then thank him for the wonderful gift."

"Thanks, Mitch." The boy's shoulders were shaking.

"What's wrong, buddy?"

"Nothing," he said, but it came out muffled.

At this juncture Mitch was racking his brain to figure him out. On impulse he said, "Don't you have a bike?"

"Yes." Zack finally lifted his tearstained face. "But it's got training wheels and I don't know how to ride it without them."

That pretty well explained everything. "You don't need training wheels. I'll show you how to ride your bike."

"You will?"

The hope in his eyes reminded Mitch of himself when he was a boy, always having to wait for someone to show him how to do things when they didn't want to.

"Of course. It'll take about fifteen minutes. After that you'll be cruising around the neighborhood with your friends and using your walkie-talkies."

Zack jumped up. "Will you show me tonight?"

"There's nothing I'd like more, but that's up to your mother." Mitch darted Heidi a glance.

"Mom? Come on! Let's go home."

Heidi looked frantic. "Are you sure you have the time, Mitch?"

That wasn't all she was asking. He sensed she was afraid. That was because their relationship was moving in a direction over which she felt she had no control. Mitch had news for her. He'd been feeling out of control since the moment Roman had introduced them at the office.

"I can spare an hour if we leave now. I'll follow you to your house."

"Th-that's very kind of you," she stammered.

Zack scrambled out of the booth clutching his present tightly. Heidi caught up to him. Mitch put some money on the table and followed them out of the restaurant to their respective cars parked in front of the firm.

En route to her house, they passed a church with a big flat parking area in the back, the perfect place for Zack to practice. When they reached her street, he followed her into the driveway of the charming, white-brick rambler. He'd been over here before, but not in daylight.

It had pale aqua shutters and cut-out window boxes full of orange-and-pink flowers. Their design was reminiscent of those he'd seen in the Swiss and Austrian Tyrol when he'd vacationed in Europe on leave from the military.

Mitch drove up behind them and waited until they'd brought Zack's bike and helmet out of the garage. He retrieved his tool kit from the trunk of his car so he could remove the training wheels. "I'll put your bike in the back of my car and we'll drive around the corner to the church. You'd better go with your mom because she has the car seat for you. Does that sound okay?"

Zack nodded with excitement.

"I'll follow you," Heidi told him. "In case you were wondering, he wouldn't let me or my brother teach him."

"I know how he feels. A guy wants his own father at a time like this. Barring that, I guess an ex-Marine will do."

She studied his features for a moment. "If anyone understands, you do. I can't thank you enough for your generosity to him."

"Let's hope I'm a good teacher."

"The thought never crossed my mind you could be anything else." With a smile he felt permeate his body, she turned away to get in her car.

He backed out and drove to the church. The sun wouldn't be setting for a while. They had enough time for Zack to get the hang of cycling before Heidi took him home to bed.

When Mitch had left TOSH the other morning, he couldn't have imagined what was awaiting him back at the office. Since meeting Heidi and her son, his world had undergone a dramatic shift.

HEIDI STOOD AGAINST THE front of her car to watch. Zack fell off his red bike several times, but Mitch was right there to help him get up and try again. It took exactly twenty minutes before Zack was riding around the parking lot by himself. "Mom! Look at me! I can ride my bike!" Joy burst out of him.

"I'm looking!" she shouted back. "That's terrific, honey!" She couldn't believe how much they looked like father and son from a distance. Zack was a little taller than average for his age and they both had the same dark-blond hair. Anyone seeing them would think they belonged to each other.

Soon Zack rode up to the Nissan with Mitch jogging alongside him to make sure no fall happened at the last second. Both faces were wreathed in smiles. Mitch held on to the bike as Zack got off and ran into her arms. She leaned down to hug and kiss him. "You did it! I'm so proud of you."

Over his shoulder she looked up at the man who'd just made her son's day and mouthed a *thank-you. You're welcome,* he mouthed back. He looked like he'd had a good time, too.

"Mitch is going to show me how to attach my walkie-talkie." Her son was so happy he seemed to have grown another inch.

"Not tonight, honey. You've got school in the morning. We need to get you home."

"Your mom's right," Mitch said before the protests could start. He put the bike in the back of his car. "We'll take care of that tomorrow."

Tomorrow? A little thrill passed through her.

"But before we leave here, I'll show you how the

walkie-talkies work. Tonight you can send messages
to your mom from your bedroom."

"Yay! They're in the car. I'll get them!"

Quick as a wink Zack reached into the back of the
Nissan, grabbed his present and gave it to Mitch. In
another couple of minutes he'd set them to the same
channel frequency and the two guys walked around
talking and saying things like "Roger" and "Over and
out." Heidi knew for a fact her son had never had such
a marvelous time. Thanks to Mitch, his confidence
level was over the top.

Mitch finally wandered up to her and handed her a
walkie-talkie. The brush of his fingers was like touching a live wire. Maybe the contact had affected him,
too, because his eyes seemed to go an even darker
brown as they met hers. "Press this button and hold it
down while you talk. If you press this other button, it
acts as a loudspeaker."

"It's easy, Mom."

She pressed both buttons and said, "Now hear this.
Now hear this." The speaker was powerful. If anyone
else had come into the parking lot, they'd have heard
it. "This is Special Agent 409."

Mitch's shoulders shook with silent laughter. 409
was a spray cleaner a lot of people used around the
house. "An all-points bulletin has gone out for a six-
year-old boy who should be home getting his bath. If
you see this individual, report in. He has blond hair
and blue eyes and answers to the name Zackatron."

Peals of laughter broke from both males. Mitch
pressed his own speaker button. "Roger and copy, 409.
This is Field Marshal X12." A popular bug spray. "I
have Zackatron in my sights."

"Excellent, Field Marshal X12." Heidi wondered if he'd been assigned a real number as a marshal. "Please deliver him immediately. Over and out." With a grin she couldn't prevent, she handed her son the walkie-talkie.

"I don't want to go home yet," he wailed.

"I know you don't. Sometimes I don't like to do things, either, like scrub the bathroom, but certain tasks have to get done and you *have* to go to school. Can you thank Mitch for teaching you how to ride and feeding us pizza and giving you these walkie-talkies? You're the luckiest boy I know."

Zack nodded before looking up at Mitch with all the signs of hero worship. "Thanks for everything, Mitch." In the next instant he did something unprecedented and hugged him.

Heidi's heart melted as she watched Mitch pick up her son and give him a big hug back. "Good job," he said before putting him down again. She knew Zack was hungry for a father's love, but seeing him show it so openly really shook her. "I had more fun than you did." Mitch handed him the other walkie-talkie.

"No, you didn't."

"Yes, I did," Mitch came back, sending her son into a giggle fit. "Go on and get in the car with your mom. I'll follow you home with your bike."

In a few minutes they were back at her house. She pressed the remote to let them in the garage. Mitch carried the bike inside and rested it against the wall next to her mountain bike. "Nice," he said.

"Hurry and get your bath started, Zack. I'll be right in."

"Okay. See ya tomorrow, Mitch."

"See you, sport."

After Zack disappeared into the house, she turned to the incredible man who'd helped her son over a very rocky patch. "I don't know how to thank you."

He cocked his head. "Do you have any idea how much fun I've had *all* day?" She didn't miss the emphasis. "If you want to know the truth, I felt just like Zack. When you said it was time to go home, I didn't want it to end, either."

Make that three people.

Mitch was getting to her in ways she was scared to examine. He was a P.I. whose firm had been hired by Bruno to find out what was going on at Bauer's. But already he was coming to mean much more than that to Heidi. She needed to remember why he was in her life at all. "What can I do to help you tomorrow?"

"Anything you'd like. Just don't go near your office or the plant. After I've entered the facility to install the devices over the lunch hour, I'll phone you and we'll go from there. Expect a call around two."

He turned to leave, then looked back over his broad shoulder. His eyes appeared black in the fading light. "For what it's worth, I think your ex-husband had to have been out of his mind to leave you and Zack."

Mitch shouldn't have told her that. Particularly since she knew he'd be leaving Salt Lake soon.

AT QUARTER TO TWELVE, Mitch put on a firefighter's uniform and climbed onto a truck from the Davis County Fire Department. Roman had arranged for their cooperation. When the truck pulled into the parking area of the Bauer plant in Woods Cross, Mitch jumped down with the three firefighters assigned to this engine and they approached the main entrance.

Earlier that morning Mitch had been on the phone to Bruno, who'd said he would tell his secretary to open the front doors for them before she went to lunch. The minute the building was cleared, the three men got busy doing their official inspection while Mitch started installing cameras in each area.

It was a medium-size facility. Everything looked immaculate. When Mitch found Jonas Bauer's office, he put in a camera, then looked around for a spot to place the listening device. There was a pot of fake flowers on an end table. Perfect!

Since there were no papers in the in-box, he opened the file cabinet with a device and went through the contents. He found some past email printouts of the shipments and studied the contents before heading for Lucas's office two doors down the hall. Once there he installed a camera and put a listening device in another fake plant on top of the file cabinet. Mitch studied the contents of his file cabinet, too.

Within the hour, the fire department had accomplished their work. Mitch walked out to the fire truck with the guys and they drove back to the station. After removing the borrowed uniform, Mitch thanked them for their help and got in his own car.

Lyle and Adam, two of the crew he'd worked with many times before, were handling surveillance of the facility in one of the firm's vans loaded with the latest state-of-the-art electronic equipment. After briefing them on the case, Mitch had asked them to park off the road behind a thick bank of trees on the east side of the plant. As he drew alongside them, he was pleased to see that the van was invisible from the road.

He climbed out of the Audi and into the van. "The deed is done, guys. It's one-thirty. People should be filing back in."

They watched the screens. One of them displayed the view of the parking lot. Like an army of worker bees, the employees converged on the scene and returned to their jobs. Within twenty minutes the place was a hive of activity. "No sign of the queen bee yet," Lyle murmured.

"Jonas could be anywhere. For that matter, so could Lucas. It might be a while before anything of importance happens." Mitch reached for the door handle. "I'm going out to take pictures of every license plate in the parking lot and get Tom to do the background checks. I'm anxious to nail the culprits.

"If anyone else drives in after I've gone, make a note of it. The camera will catch it and we'll blow it up later to get the license plate number. Jeff and Phil will relieve you at midnight. Stay in contact with me."

"Will do."

After Mitch had driven around getting pictures, he sent them through his iPhone to Tom, then headed for Salt Lake and phoned Heidi. His pulse accelerated while he waited for her to answer.

"How did everything go?" she asked as soon as she picked up.

"Without a hitch. My spy gadgets are in place. Too bad Zack isn't older. He could've helped me. What are you doing right now?"

"I'm on my way to pick him up from school. Before

that I was pulling some weeds around the side of the house, but I'll never do it again in this heat."

"It's a scorcher today." He switched lanes. "Why don't I drop by your house and I'll put that walkie-talkie on his bike?"

"My son will be thrilled."

And you? "Then I'll see you in a half hour."

Coming into Salt Lake, he took the Sixth South exit and headed home. On the way he stopped at Emigration Cyclery on Foothill Drive. They had an array of mountain bikes. Seeing Heidi's bike in her garage last evening had given him an idea. He bought a bike and put it in the back of his Audi. Now that he had full use of his arm, he could resume activities he'd enjoyed before the shooting. His old bike was still in storage back in Florida.

One of the college girls from next door saw his new purchase when he pulled into the carport. She and her roommate cycled a lot and she wanted to ride with him, but Mitch had other plans. For one thing, both girls were too young. And even if they weren't, his interest was engaged elsewhere.

As politely as he knew how, he told her he was running late and would have to talk to her another time. On that note he hurried through the apartment to change into shorts and a T-shirt. He had plans to be with the two people who'd changed his world.

Chapter Five

"Mom!" Zack came running into the house. He was already wearing his helmet. "Mitch is here." Heidi's son had been watching for his hero. "He brought his bike!"

She realized Mitch was offering himself as a stand-in because Zack didn't have a friend to ride with right now. Heidi was learning fast that he was a caring, sensitive man. She decided his being raised by a succession of foster and not his biological parents didn't matter. Mitch had been *born* with qualities a lot of people lacked, including her ex-husband.

Without hesitation she hurried through the house to the front porch. What she saw was a modern-day version of a golden god helping Zack attach his walkie-talkie to his bike. Those were her own words this time, not ones her sister, Evy, might have said.

Mitch lifted his head. "Hi," he said as his gaze swept over her. "Is it all right with you if we ride to the church from here and test out our walkie-talkies? Then we'll come back."

"Of course."

With Mitch's help getting started, Zack started down the street. "Bye, Mom," he called over his shoulder. Mitch put on his own helmet before getting on his bike. He caught up to Zack with the agility of a man in amazing shape, considering he'd been recovering from a bullet wound all this time. She longed to go with them.

As soon as they disappeared around the corner, she dashed into the house and pulled on a pair of shorts and a knit top. Once her sneakers were tied, she locked the front door and hurried to the garage for her bike and helmet. In minutes she was flying down the driveway.

She felt like a little kid again, hurrying to meet up with friends. But she was a woman now and none of the boys on her old block had looked like the hard-muscled male racing around the church parking lot with her son. Heidi pedaled hard to catch up with them. When she did, she asked Zack, "Mind if I help hunt for bad guys, Zackatron?"

Her son pressed the speaker button on his device. "We're looking for stolen cars, Agent 409." Zack stepped right into the mood of the moment.

Her gaze darted to Mitch, who was grinning. "No luck yet," he said into his speaker. "Any suggestions?"

"Maybe we'll see some at the convenience store. Zackatron knows where it is."

"Yup. Follow me."

It didn't take long before they were drinking icy slurpees. Mitch finished his off fast. "That tasted good, but I'm getting hungry for dinner. I only live four blocks from here. Would you two spies like to come to my apartment? We'll throw some hot dogs on the grill and roast marshmallows afterward to make s'mores."

Zack's head whipped around toward her. "Could we, Mom? Please?"

This was her fault. If she hadn't joined them, she wouldn't be in the position to play the bad guy by refusing Mitch's invitation. She didn't have a reason to say no. In truth, she didn't want to. But if she accepted, it meant she'd crossed way beyond the line into territory where she was vulnerable and could be hurt again.

Unfortunately the pleading in Zack's eyes overrode her caution. He was very vulnerable right now, too, yet she had to admit this man was boosting her son's belief in himself. You couldn't buy that kind of help.

"I think it sounds like fun. We'd love a barbecue."

"Yay!"

A satisfied gleam entered Mitch's eyes. "You took the words right out of my mouth, sport. Let's go."

Zack was growing proficient at climbing on his bike and taking off by himself. Heidi was secretly delighted with his progress. It was all due to this man whose intention to infiltrate the company had somehow spilled into her private life, as well. *With her permission.*

She and Zack followed Mitch onto a side street that avoided the heavy traffic on Foothill Drive and cut through the residential area to his apartment complex. How many years had she driven past it on her way to the zoo or up the canyon? He'd been living here almost a year without her knowledge. The chances of their homes being this close to each other were probably a million to one.

Mitch headed for the third carport and hopped off. "We can leave our bikes here." They took off their helmets, then he unlocked the door and ushered them into the kitchen. "Welcome to my abode. Normally the management only rents to college students, but an exception was made for me. The bathroom is down the hall on the left."

Mitch had been well hidden. With the killer still on the loose looking for him, the chances of him being tracked down clear across the country weren't that great. Furthermore no one would think to look for him in a housing complex meant for college students. But that didn't ease Heidi's fears. They lurked in the back of her mind and came out of hiding at odd moments.

"Come on, Zack," she said. "Let's go wash our hands."

His apartment was tiny, but thankfully it had good air-conditioning. Only two small bedrooms, a bathroom, a living room and kitchen with a small dinette set. The unoccupied bedroom was filled with fitness equipment. Zack noticed it before they rejoined Mitch on the veranda off the kitchen, where he was heating up the grill.

There were four deck chairs surrounding a round glass table with an umbrella. He'd pulled down an awning to shade them from the sun. It wouldn't fall below the Great Salt Lake for another hour at least.

Mitch's glance took in both of them. "When I'm home and not sleeping, this is my favorite room in the house."

She nodded. "It would be mine, too."

"This porch isn't a room," Zack said.

A chuckle escaped Mitch's lips. "It is for me. Want to help?"

"We both do," Heidi chimed in.

They worked in harmony. Zack set the table with

paper plates, potato chips and condiments. Mitch started the hot dogs and Heidi tossed a green salad with the ingredients he had on hand. She fixed her own version of Thousand Island dressing. By then Mitch had made up a pitcher of lemonade and soon they were ready to eat.

"After dinner can I play with some of the stuff in the second bedroom?"

Mitch was working on his third hot dog. She was pleased to note he'd had several helpings of salad with liberal portions of her dressing. He'd already complimented her on it. "You mean the treadmill and exercise bike?"

"Yeah."

"I have a better idea. If you want to come over on Saturday, we'll do a real workout when we're not starving and hot."

"Okay! That's how come you're so strong, huh?"

"The machines help, especially when I have to work odd hours sometimes. But I much prefer going for a bike ride outside. It keeps you in great shape. Now that you can ride your bike, you'll build lots of muscles and it's good for your heart. You know, you're lucky to live in Salt Lake where you can ride your bike outdoors almost year round."

Zack stop munching on his potato chip. "*You* live here, too."

"I do right now."

Heidi schooled her features not to react, but her son's little face fell on cue. "How come not all the time?"

"Mitch's home is in Florida," she interjected, not wanting to let this discussion go any further. But she decided it was best he knew the truth. "Mitch is only working here temporarily." She switched subjects. "Hey, guys, I don't know about you, but I'm hungry for a s'more."

Their host got up from the table before she could. Whatever was on his mind had put an expression on his face that puzzled her. "I'll bring everything out."

"Come on, Zack," Heidi said. "Let's clear the table."

In a few minutes they were cooking marshmallows over the grill with fondue forks. Heidi put them between graham crackers and chocolate. Soon they'd devoured everything, with Mitch pronounced grand champion for eating the most.

"Speaking of champions, have you ever watched the Tour de France, Zack?"

"What's that?"

His mouth curved upward. "A big bike race in France that lasts three weeks."

His eyebrows lifted. "That long?"

"They don't ride continuously. Every day they cover a certain section of the route, then they go to bed in the town they come to. The next day they get up and eat, and then ride the next section."

"What if it rains?"

"They ride through anything. Rain, wind, snow."

"Snow?"

"That's right. Their route might start in a valley. But when they have to climb to the summit of a mountain, they sometimes end up in a snowstorm."

"Don't they get cold?"

"Yup. They get cold and hot and have to layer their clothes for every eventuality. Just two days ago they biked through snow. But you have to realize these guys

are in fabulous shape. A few of them are Americans.
The race is going on right now. I've been recording the
stages. Want to see a little bit of it?"

"Yeah!"

After a quick cleanup, all three trooped into the
living room and sat down on the couch and love seat.
For the next half hour they watched the last third of
the day's race while Mitch patiently explained the as-
pects including the significance of the peloton.

"Wow!" Zack exclaimed as he watched the cyclists climb a twisting road. "That road winds up like
a snake!"

Mitch nodded. "It does. Look at that one poor rider
at the back. He's lost his legs. He's starting to wobble."

"Just like the zombies in the video game."

"Exactly like that. Uh-oh. Someone crashed."

"Why do they get so close?"

"The first guy faces the wind. The guy close behind
him doesn't have to work as hard. They plan every
move to conserve their energy until they try to make
a break and become the leader."

"The scenery is stupendous," Heidi said. "Oh, it
makes me want to go back there so badly I can hardly
stand it. There's no scenery like it in the world."

"You've been there?" Zack sounded incredulous.

"Yes. With a bunch of friends while I was in college."

"I didn't know that." He jerked his head toward
Mitch. "Have *you* been there?"

He nodded. "Several times when I was on leave
from the military. A couple of my friends and I rented
a car and drove through a part of the French Alps." As
he spoke to Zack, his gaze met hers. "I agree there's

no place like it. Those cyclists climb the summits like mountain goats."

Heidi expelled a sigh. "I don't know how they manage those climbs day after day. They're *iron* men."

Zack thought that was funny and laughed. Then he suddenly blurted, "Hey, Mom, look at that cool castle!"

"Europe's full of them. When you're a little older, I'm going to take us there. I want you to see Austria and England."

"England?"

"Yes. Your Grandma Bauer was a Taylor before she got married. The Taylor family is from the Isle of Wight. You have an ancestor, Thomas Taylor, who was a pioneer. He lived in a town with a huge castle. When we explore it you'll be able to spy like crazy through dark passages and dungeons and watch towers."

Her son's eyes were still glued on the racers. "Maybe I could ride in that race when I'm older! And at night I could sleep in one of those castles."

"Anything's possible." Her eyes met Mitch's and they both chuckled quietly. Zack had only learned how to ride his bike yesterday.

Once they'd watched the French rider climb today's podium and put on the yellow jersey, Heidi stood up. "Guess what, honey? It's time to go home. You've got school in the morning."

Following that thought, she realized Mitch would be starting work in the warehouse. They wouldn't have this kind of togetherness anymore. And soon he'd find out what was going on inside the plant. Then he'd leave for Florida, taking all the excitement and wonder of this week with him. How was she going to handle that?

She didn't even want to think about Zack's reaction when he learned Mitch was gone.

Their host turned off the TV. "The sun's gone down. Our ride back to your house won't be so hot now."

"I wish we didn't have to go."

Oh, Zack. I'm with you on that, honey.

She put her arm on his shoulder as they walked him out to the carport. "Even spies need their sleep, no matter how old. Isn't that right, Agent X12?"

Mitch shot her a piercing glance. "Right." He adjusted his own helmet strap. The man was so handsome, Heidi forgot not to stare. But she had to remember he would be on a huge spy mission starting tomorrow morning. Just thinking about it made her tremble for whoever was stealing from the company.

They would have no idea Mitch was on to them until it was too late. So far she and Zack had only seen the thrilling part of him, but she knew deep down he had a forbidding side when he went in pursuit.

AT FIVE TO EIGHT THE NEXT morning, Mitch reported for work at the Bauer's plant in Woods Cross. As per Heidi's instructions, he wore a dark blue polo shirt and khaki shorts. He'd already stopped by the surveillance van to pick up all the tapes to study later.

The receptionist in the plant told him to be seated. Over the loudspeaker she called for Randy to come to the front desk. Mitch had memorized the names of the people in charge. Randy Pierson was the Bauer who'd be Mitch's shift boss.

In a few minutes a blond guy in a similar blue polo shirt and khaki shorts appeared and shook Mitch's hand. "Welcome to the company, Mr. Garrett. I can see Ms. Norris prepared you and sent me a copy of your file. I'm Randy. Mind if I call you Mitch? We're not formal around here."

"I'd prefer it."

"Great. I was told we'd be getting a new man today. You'll like it here." Randy, who looked to be around Mitch's age, seemed an affable fellow.

"I'm looking forward to it."

"I'll show you around. When we finish today, you can put in an order for the polos we wear. You should have those shirts by Tuesday of next week. Come with me."

While Randy explained the schedule and the breaks, they toured the premises Mitch had covered by himself yesterday. They ended up in the warehouse and truck-bay area located at the south end of the plant.

"Let me introduce you to the man you'll be working with." They walked out to the loading dock where a truck had backed in.

"Harold? Come here a minute."

A middle-aged man with thinning brown hair and a barrel chest pushed an empty dolly down the ramp and walked toward them. "Where's Jack?" he said. "We've got a lot to load this morning."

"I've been told he wanted to train for a SweetSpuds manager job in one of the shops. This is Mitch Garrett, his replacement."

Harold didn't look too happy, but he shook hands with Mitch, sizing him up. "Ever done any warehouse work before?"

"No."

"Mitch will be working with you, Harold. Show

him the ropes. If you need anything, just come by my office."

"Will do. Thanks, Randy."

As he walked away, Harold squinted at Mitch. "I can't figure out how come you got Jack's job. There are guys in other parts of the plant who've been waiting years to work here. Are you a Bauer?"

Naturally that was the man's first question. "No." *But I'm crazy about a couple of them.*

"What kind of work have you done?"

"I'm just out of the Marines."

"Marines, huh?" He eyed Mitch once more. "Do you know anything about Bauer's?"

"I've been in orientation all week."

He nodded. "Okay. See these motor-driven carts?"

"Yeah?"

"They're piled with bags of donut mix the guys from the mix area loaded yesterday. See this card here?" He pointed to a yellow, eight-by-ten piece of cardboard sticking out beneath one of the bags with the number three hundred on it.

Mitch nodded.

"When we put these bags on the truck and lift the bag off that card, it will have their destination. They've already been counted, but we'll do it again to make sure it's the right amount. Then we'll push the slider against the shipment and fasten the strap. Before you start more loading, you stick the yellow card in the slot on the back of the slider so the destination is clear."

"Got it." So far Mitch couldn't find anything wrong with the unique system that checked the load twice. The problem lay with the culprits who were stealing the merchandise.

"Load as many as you can onto this dolly and push it up the ramp into the truck all the way to the end. Thirty-two bags across from roof to floor make one row. How many are we loading?"

"Three hundred."

"That makes how many rows?"

"Ten."

"Then start counting." Harold had all the makings of a drill sergeant. Mitch got busy while Harold kept an eagle eye on him and followed him inside. When they reached the back of the truck, Mitch could see his partner had already done a row of four stacks. Nine more rows to go.

"Start filling up another row just like it."

"Yes, sir."

Mitch got busy. As he loaded the next row, he checked the ends of the bags that had already been loaded. No red tags. He called out the number of the row every time he finished one. Harold probably didn't like that, either, but Mitch didn't want to give him any reason to tell him he wasn't up to the job.

The rest of the time they worked in silence. During the process Mitch checked the bottom seams of each bag looking for red tags among the blue. He found five before Harold pushed the slider against the row and attached the strap.

Harold finally spoke again, handing Mitch the yellow card. "Okay." It said San Francisco. "Put the card in the pocket on the back of the slider." Mitch did as he was told. "Now we'll keep loading until it's full, then we'll eat lunch. After that we'll load one more truck. Your shift will be over at four-thirty."

Randy had already given Mitch the drill, but Mitch

didn't say anything because it was obvious Harold was the type who liked to feel important. They worked steadily until noon. Mitch had checked every bag. All in all, twenty-five bags of mix had been switched for flour on this truckload headed to San Francisco through Elko and Reno.

Without saying anything to Mitch, Harold made his way to Randy's office and went in. After a moment the two came out. Randy checked off the shipment on his clipboard. "How's it going, Mitch?"

"Good. Everything's straightforward. Harold's an excellent trainer." For now every person in the plant was suspect in Mitch's eyes.

Randy smiled at Harold. "We couldn't get along without him." That comment didn't seem to please Harold at all. Maybe it felt patronizing. Mitch didn't know. "Enjoy your lunch, guys."

After Randy excused himself, Harold took off. That gave Mitch the freedom to go out to his car. In another minute he met up with his crew in the surveillance van. They had a hamburger and fries waiting for him. He washed his hands before eating with them.

"I counted twenty-five bags of flour on that shipment we loaded. If Harold's in on it, I'm convinced that's why he's so upset his partner was replaced. At the moment you could say he doesn't like working with me. If he doesn't know about the thefts, then he's just a bitter man."

Adam grinned. "You kept one step ahead of him. It probably bugged him, but that back of yours is going to be aching by tonight. I groaned every time you bent over. How's your arm?"

"I'm supposed to be a hundred percent. So far, so

good." He gobbled his food while he looked at the various screens. "I'll be loading another truck this afternoon. If Bruno hadn't recovered from his stroke well enough for his friend to tell him what was going on here, this kind of crime could have gone on indefinitely."

"Do you get any vibes from the guy with the clipboard?"

"Randy's nice and friendly, but maybe it's a cover. One thing I've noticed. Only Harold and I were doing the counting of the bags. Randy just checked the load off at the end. There was no sign of Lucas, who's supposed to be in charge of quality control. I understood he does it while the carts are loaded. I'll find out more when I go over the tapes tonight."

"Don't kill yourself out there and ruin that arm, Mitch."

"I'm all right." He downed the rest of his Coke. "Now I've got to go." He thanked the guys and drove back to the plant to start his afternoon shift. The truck they'd loaded had already left the bay and a new one stood parked at the dock ready to load.

Harold joined him as he was putting the last bag on the dolly before starting to fill up the truck. "Who are you trying to impress?"

Just for fun Mitch flashed him a quick smile. "You."

Harold wasn't amused. "Eager beavers can wear out fast."

"Would you like me to slow down? Just say the word."

The other man frowned before turning away and getting to work. For the rest of the afternoon they loaded shipments for San Diego, California, through

Las Vegas and Utah. So far no bags of flour were in the bunch, but he still had a hundred more bags to load before the truck was full.

Suddenly his adrenaline surged. Fifty of the last hundred bags had *red* tags. Something different was going on with this truckload. Maybe because the thieves hadn't been caught yet, they'd grown more daring. While he piled the last of the bags onto the dolly, Harold again made his way to Randy's office.

Mitch worked the slider and shoved it around. According to the yellow card, this last load of two hundred and fifty bags was headed for Beaver, Utah, a small town a couple of hours south of Woods Cross. He attached the strap and put the card in the pocket. With the truck loaded, he set the dolly against the side wall and walked down the ramp.

Once more Randy came out of his office and checked off the shipment. He flicked Mitch and Harold a friendly glance. "Great job today. In case you've forgotten, we're closed for the twenty-fourth on Monday because of Pioneer Day. See you on Tuesday morning."

"Thanks for the reminder, Randy. Good night," he said to both of them.

Mitch hurried out of the plant to his car and drove it to the surveillance van. Once inside, he changed into a T-shirt and jeans. "I made a fascinating new discovery, guys." He put his New York Yankees baseball cap on backward. "The truck you'll see leaving in a few minutes is headed for Beaver, ostensibly with an order of two hundred and fifty bags of mix. But fifty of the bags are flour."

Lyle let out a whistle. "Why are they stealing the flour?"

"Who knows? I'm going to follow it and see what happens. I might need backup."

"Phil's available."

"Good. Tell him to get down to I-15 on Thirty-third South and wait to hear from me."

"We're on it."

"Keep your eyes on the storage rooms. The switches will be happening pretty soon. Lucas is supposed to count the bags loaded on the carts. You've been given pictures of the main players and will be able to spot him if he's there doing his job. Let me know."

"Will do."

He got back in his car and called Roman to give him a progress report. Just as he disconnected, he saw the Bauer truck head for the entrance to the freeway headed south. He switched on the ignition and followed.

"Mom? Can we drive to Tim's with my bike? I want to cycle with him."

Now that school was over for the week, Heidi was glad he had someone else on his mind besides Mitch. She couldn't say the same for herself. Mitch had been working at the plant all day. She was anxious to know what he'd found out. More than that, she was eager to hear his voice.

"Sure, but before we go, we need to have a little talk."

His blue eyes fastened on her. "Am I in trouble?"

She chuckled. "No, honey. But if anyone should ask, just tell them a guy in our neighborhood helped you learn to ride without your training wheels. Don't mention that Mitch has been training with the company."

"How come?"

"Because it's temporary and pretty soon he'll be going back to Florida."

A frown appeared. "How come?"

"It's his home, remember?"

"Oh, yeah." He looked downcast. "Do you like Mitch?"

"Of course."

"Me, too." No kidding. "I wish he didn't have to leave."

Heidi gave him a kiss on the forehead to cover her feelings, then phoned Sharon to make the arrangements. Before long Zack and Tim were cruising around his neighborhood using the walkie-talkies. While her sister-in-law was getting dinner ready for her family, Heidi volunteered to watch the kids from the front porch.

Later Sharon came outside. "When did the training wheels come off?"

"A couple of days ag— Uh-oh, that's my phone. I'd better get it." Saved by the bell. Heidi reached into her purse for her cell and clicked on. "Hello?"

"I'm glad you picked up." Mitch's voice.

Since Sharon was within earshot, Heidi had to improvise. "Hi! What's the verdict on Jim?"

"Obviously you can't talk. Call me when you can." He disconnected. Mitch was all business, letting her know something serious was going on.

She gripped her phone tighter. "That's good news, Phyllis. Thanks for letting me know. Bye." Heidi clicked off.

"What was that about?"

"Work. Jim's the baker at the Foothill Shop. He

doesn't have to go in for surgery, after all. Now I won't have to find a substitute."

"One less headache for you."

"You're right."

"Are you sure you won't stay for dinner?"

"You're sweet, but tonight Zack wants me to watch the *Clone Wars* with him on TV. The show will be starting in a half hour. Thanks, anyway."

After hugging Sharon, she called to Zack, who came speeding up the driveway. Once they put his bike in the trunk, they were ready to go.

"See ya, Tim."

"See ya, Zack." He handed him the walkie-talkie.

On their way home, she darted her son a glance. "I bet Tim was surprised."

"He couldn't believe it. I told him Mitch gave me the walkie-talkies, too. He wants to go to that spy shop."

Oh, dear. "Who wouldn't? Did you guys have a good time?"

"Yes, but he's not as fun as Mitch."

Nope. Heidi was fast discovering there was no one like Mitch.

"Do you think he could come over to our house tonight and watch the bike race with us?"

"Not tonight."

"Why not?"

"He's still at work."

Once they were back home, she told him to wash his hands while she fixed fruit salad and homemade corn dogs for their dinner. While he was occupied, she called Mitch, but all she got was his voice mail. Whatever he was doing, he'd sounded intense earlier.

While she was fixing dinner, the phone rang again. She grabbed it. "Mitch?"

"No," sounded another familiar voice. "It's your mom. I've got the speaker on so your father can hear us, too."

"Oh, hi!" she exclaimed, hardly able to think. "I thought it was someone else. Are you two already home? I assumed you wouldn't get back before tomorrow."

"We're just leaving Rock Springs, Wyoming, and ought to be in Salt Lake in about three hours. It'll be too late for you to come over to the house, so we thought we'd call and see how you are."

"Zack and I are fine." That was the understatement of the century. "How are you? How's Evy?"

"Everyone's great and little Stacy is adorable."

"I can't wait to see this new baby."

"They promised to come for Thanksgi—"

"Mom—" Zack came bounding in the kitchen, breaking in on the conversation "—is that Mitch?" Heidi's mother couldn't have failed to hear him.

She turned her head toward him. "It's your grandma. Do you remember we don't talk when we see one of us is on the phone?"

"I forgot. Are they home?"

She gave up. "They will be later tonight."

"Can I talk to her?"

Heidi handed him her cell. She already knew what he was going to tell his grandparents. For the next minute they couldn't get a word in edgewise as he rhapsodized over his experiences with Mitch. Now that he'd been exposed to the world of the Tour de France, he couldn't talk enough about it or the man who'd breathed confidence into him without even trying.

"I love you, too, Grandma. Here's Mom." He handed her the phone. "Hurry. The *Clone Wars* are going to start and then I want to watch and see if any more guys crash their bikes in the race."

"Not until you sit down and eat." She took a deep breath, then said, "Hi, Mom."

"Hi. I can't decide who sounded more excited when they thought it was Mitch."

Heidi felt her face go hot. "Does he have a last name?"

"Yes. It's Garrett. He's the P.I.," she whispered so that Zack wouldn't hear. As far as she knew her parents had never kept secrets from each other, so she had to assume her mother knew about the thefts. If she didn't, then her mom would ask Heidi's father when they hung up. "Tell you what. As soon as I've fed Zack, I'll call you back. I promise."

MITCH WOULD HAVE ANSWERED Heidi's phone call, but the truck driver had suddenly switched lanes and taken the turn off for Draper, one of the communities in South Salt Lake. He'd only been on the road about forty minutes. Heidi said the trucks were gassed up every time they left the bay, so maybe the driver was stopping for dinner and a bathroom break.

Or maybe he wasn't.

The driver turned left and took several roads before coming to a medium-size storage facility. He knew the combination to get in because the gate opened from the side before closing again. The office wasn't closed yet. Mitch parked his car and went in, asking if he could rent a shed. When the paperwork was done, he was given the key and the combination to the gate before going back outside.

Phil, from Lufka, had pulled up next to his car. Mitch walked over to him. "I'm going in with my car. If by any chance I miss the truck, you follow it and I'll catch up." Phil nodded.

Once inside, Mitch drove around the mazelike facility until he spied the Bauer truck at one end of the K section in front of the last shed. Next to it was an older dark blue pickup. Three guys, all in their twenties, were moving bags from the truck into the pickup as fast as they could. Mitch pulled out his binoculars, but didn't recognize any of them from the application photos.

They hadn't opened any of the shed doors. Mitch wondered if the storage sheds were even being used, but he would come back later to find out. This was the perfect spot to transfer the bags where no one would think anything about it. He filmed them for a minute, then drove out to join Phil.

"What's up?"

"Before long you'll see a blue pickup with three guys come through the gate. They've taken a bunch of bags from off the truck. I'll follow them while you wait for the Bauer truck. See where it stops next, then call me. If you need backup, holler."

No sooner had he gotten back in his car when the big truck left the facility first and started down the road for the freeway. He exchanged glances with Phil who took off after it. It was five minutes before the pickup appeared. All three guys rode in front.

First they stopped at a drive-thru. Mitch was right

behind them and ordered a sandwich. He phoned in the license plate number to Lon, a retired police officer who worked for Lufkas. He would find out the information. Next, the pickup drove out to the freeway and headed south. When it took the Alpine turn off five minutes later, Mitch called Phil.

"Are you in Alpine, too?"

"No. The truck's headed due south at a fast clip."

"If it's supposed to be in Beaver by a certain time, I'm not surprised the driver is trying to make up for lost time at the storage place. Don't follow it past its next stop, since we know the rest of the shipments haven't been switched. Stay in touch."

"Ditto."

Mitch checked Alpine's population on his iPhone. 9500 inhabitants. If there was a Bauer outlet here, then this stop hadn't been put on the normal schedule. But the Bauer truck driver knew to stop in Draper at the storage rental to make a delivery. Was the driver acting on his own? Or was he following orders from the mastermind of this scheme?

Full of questions, Mitch followed the pickup to the business center. When they came to a small strip mall with a variety of shops still open, they drove around to the alley behind it and stopped at the center shop so the tailgate faced the door.

Someone from inside the shop opened the door for them. Quickly the driver lowered the tailgate and climbed in the truck bed. He began handing bags to the others, who carried them inside. Mitch had parked near some other cars and got it all on film. Once the load had been delivered, the guy from the shop shut the door and the three guys all got back in the pickup.

The pickup then went to a supermarket a mile away and pulled into the crowded parking lot. Two of the guys got out and walked to their own cars. Mitch took down their license plate numbers, but he stayed with the pickup and followed it for about a mile, to a small, framed house. The driver drove around the back of it.

When the pickup disappeared, Mitch noted the address, then made a U-turn and drove back to the strip mall. The center shop was called Drop In Family Pub, and it featured music, games, homemade pizza and donuts. Mitch decided this was a great time to pay a visit.

The place brought in a good crowd. He wandered inside, paid for a round of pool, then bought two donuts for takeout from the good-looking young woman at the counter. They didn't serve alcohol.

He smiled at her. "This is a great place," he said with a Southern accent. "How long y'all been in business?"

"About six months. The same time the movie complex went in down the street. Why not try our pizza, too? It's new on the menu."

"I don't know. I'm not a big pizza fan."

"This is different. Secret recipe," she confided. "I promise you'll like it."

"All right, sugar. You've talked me into it. I'll take a medium with Canadian bacon."

After she'd boxed one up for him, he winked at her. "If I like it, I'll be back."

"Don't take too long. My name's Georgia. What's yours?" A flirt, too.

"I'll tell you the next time I come in. See y'all around."

As far as he could tell, there were two other employees circulating. Both were guys in their twenties. Much as he wanted to ask more questions—like who was the owner—this wasn't the time to arouse suspicion.

He left the pub and headed back to Salt Lake. On the way he heard from Phil who'd watched the truck drop off the delivery in Beaver at the Bauer outlet. Now he was on his way back home.

Mitch told him about the pub in Alpine. After they'd talked shop, he phoned Heidi. Eight-thirty wasn't too late. Since it was a Friday, she probably hadn't put Zack to bed yet.

"Mitch?" She'd answered before the second ring. He thought he heard a tinge of anxiety in her tone. "Are you all right?"

More than all right now that he heard her voice. "I couldn't be better. What about you?"

"I'm fine." She sounded a trifle impatient. "I'm dying to hear what's been happening. I got a little worried when you didn't answer."

"I couldn't right then. Is it too late to come by your house?"

"Of course not."

"What about Zack?"

"He's in the tub. I'll be putting him to bed in a minute because he's going to see his grandparents in the morning. They'll be home late tonight. Now that you've helped him learn to ride his bike, he can't wait to show them. On the phone he told them that one day he wanted to ride in the Ter da Frants." She mimicked Zack's pronunciation of the Tour de France. "That's *your* doing."

Mitch chuckled in delight. "I'll be there in twenty minutes. I've brought food."

"I was just going to say I'd make you a homemade corn dog. That's what we had for dinner."

"What a coincidence since I'm bringing *you* something homemade. See you in a little while. I'll knock." He hung up because he knew she needed to get Zack to bed.

As his car ate up the miles, he felt as if he hadn't seen her in years. If he felt like this now, how was he going to feel when he put the distance of the country between them? The way this case was going, it would be wrapped up shortly.

When he thought of the condo in Tallahassee he'd been subletting, the idea of returning to its emptiness left him cold. But he knew Lew wanted him back there soon or he'd have to bring in another marshal. Mitch needed to make up his mind. If he wanted to stay with the marshals, he didn't want to work anywhere else in Florida except Tallahassee, otherwise...

Otherwise what, Garrett? Your mother might come looking for you and not be able to find you? Are you still hung up on that childhood dream?

Since meeting Zack, memories of Mitch's own childhood had been surfacing right and left. The boy had a fantastic mother and a strong support system that would see him happily through life. But in Zack's vulnerable moments brought on because his father wasn't around, Mitch saw himself in the boy.

How pathetic that Mitch was now thirty-four and he still hadn't let the dream go. In his gut he knew he didn't want to live in Florida. It had never felt like home. No place had ever called to him. The closest he'd ever come to such a feeling was right now as he turned into Heidi's driveway. Her garden and window boxes were a riot of color. Everywhere he looked was evidence of her handiwork.

Then he saw her standing on the front porch waiting for him.

She fulfilled him.

She thrilled him.

Chapter Six

"I can smell pizza," Heidi said as they walked into the kitchen. She was too happy to see Mitch to focus on food, but she figured he was starving.

"Before you try it, I want you to taste the dessert in this sack." She turned around, smiling up at the most appealing man she'd ever met. "Close your eyes first and keep them closed until I tell you to open them."

Mitch's mysterious behavior had aroused her curiosity. "What's this? Dessert before dinner? I don't do well on sugar before I eat."

"Neither do I, but I'm asking you to make an exception this once. Go on. Just one bite," he urged in a solemn tone.

Heidi decided she'd better close her eyes, sensing he wasn't just playing with her. He put something right against her lips. It was sweet all right. "Why did you bring me donuts?"

"Will you please stop asking questions and obey me?"

"Obey you?" She laughed "That sounds serious. All right. Because you *asked* me so nicely, I'll do it." She bit into it and chewed it before swallowing. "Mitch, I

Get 2 Books FREE!

Harlequin® Books,
publisher of women's fiction,
presents

Harlequin®

American ★ Romance®

GET 2 BOOKS

We'd like to send you two *Harlequin American Romance®* novels absolutely free. Accepting them puts you under no obligation to purchase any more books.

HOW TO GET YOUR 2 FREE BOOKS AND 2 FREE GIFTS

1. Return the reply card today, and we'll send you two *Harlequin American Romance* novels, absolutely free! We'll even pay the postage!

2. Accepting free books places you under no obligation to buy anything, ever. Whatever you decide, the free books and gifts are yours to keep, free!

3. We hope that after receiving your free books you'll want to remain a subscriber, but the choice is yours– to continue or cancel, any time at all!

EXTRA BONUS

You'll also get two free mystery gifts! (worth about $10)

FREE!

◀ **DETACH AND MAIL CARD TODAY!** ▼

If offer card is missing, write to: The Reader Service, P.O. Box 1867, Buffalo, NY 14240-1867 or visit www.ReaderService.com

BUSINESS REPLY MAIL

FIRST-CLASS MAIL   PERMIT NO. 717   BUFFALO, NY

POSTAGE WILL BE PAID BY ADDRESSEE

THE READER SERVICE
PO BOX 1867
BUFFALO NY 14240-9952

NO POSTAGE
NECESSARY
IF MAILED
IN THE
UNITED STATES

could have brought donuts home from our No. 2 store if you'd asked me. You're a tease, you know that?"

He didn't laugh back. "There's no question in your mind this is a Bauer donut?"

"None." She kept smiling. "If you're trying to trick me, it won't work. I've probably eaten hundreds of them in my lifetime and know what our donuts taste like." He was standing so close she could feel his warmth. A couple of inches more and she'd find his mouth. More than anything she wanted to taste it. She kept waiting for him to kiss her. "Do you still want me to keep my eyes closed?" The suspense was killing her.

"No. You can open them."

Something was wrong. Maybe he hadn't wanted to kiss her, after all. She felt like a fool and did his bidding.

"*This* is what you bit into."

He held up the donut she'd just taken a bite out of, but her head was still reeling from errant thoughts that had nothing to do with donuts and everything to do with taking a delicious bite out of *him.* Or him out of her, whichever came first.

Hadn't he wanted to kiss her? It was all she'd been able to think about. In her confusion she blinked. "I don't understand."

"Have you ever seen a Bauer donut that looked like this?"

He reached into the sack and pulled out another one, holding both up. They were identical. Forcing herself to concentrate, she noticed they were larger than a normal-size donut, and they had a smaller hole at the center.

She frowned. "I didn't know we were trying out a new nozzle. The idea hasn't come up in our board meetings. Whoever has been experimenting is going to be in trouble for this. Which one of our outlets sold this to you?"

"This is where the donuts came from." Mitch held up the donut sack so she could see the advertising on the front. She hadn't paid any attention to it before. He'd been the only thing to fill her vision.

Drop In Family Pub—featuring music, games, homemade pizza and donuts.
Open to all ages seven days a week, 11 to 11
Alpine, Utah

He watched her, obviously waiting for a response. All the time since he'd arrived at the house, she'd thought he'd been setting her up for a kiss because he couldn't hold back from kissing her any longer. Instead he'd been using her as a guinea pig in order to prove that the Drop In Family Pub was serving Bauer products to the public.

Disappointment consumed her for being wrong about him. She fought to recover so he'd never know what was going on inside her. A tiny gasp escaped her throat.

"You know what else I think?" His eyes bored into hers. "I think this pizza has been made with Bauer potato flour. Are you up for one more experiment?" He lifted the lid of the pizza box.

Heidi took a piece and bit into it. The consistency of the dough was lighter than that of ordinary pizza. She took several more bites before putting it down.

"I've never eaten anything like it before, but I'd have to make some pizza from scratch using the potato flour to prove this pizza was made with it."

Mitch put the donut sack on the counter. "I found out from the waitress that the pub opened six months ago. Quite an enterprise someone is running with your company's products."

Her mind was trying to put all this together. "Mitch, our company doesn't have an outlet or franchise in Alpine, Utah."

"I knew that from the information you gave me earlier. From the beginning I've wondered where the stolen mix bags had gone. Today I followed the truck I'd loaded in the afternoon. I called one of my crew to help provide backup. To my surprise, the truck driver turned off at Draper."

"What?"

"It's true. He drove to a storage facility where a pickup truck was waiting to offload the stolen bags of mix and flour. You can bet a load of fifty bags of mix and flour are dropped off at that storage facility every time a Bauer truck heads south. Once the transfer is made, the driver continues on to make official deliveries in Utah and elsewhere. Someone's got a perfect system in place."

"How does anyone dare do something like this?" She was so upset she grasped his arms, acting on impulse. But when she felt a tremor pass through his powerful body, she realized what she'd done and quickly removed her hands.

"Far too easily, I'm afraid," he answered in a husky voice.

Embarrassed by her impulsive gesture, she said,

"Tell me everything that happened today. Don't leave anything out."

"Why don't we sit down?" he murmured. "I have some videos to show you. Perhaps you'll be able to identify some of these people."

For the next half hour she watched the pictures on his iPhone, but didn't recognize anyone except the driver of the Bauer truck, Matt Sayer, who'd been with the company at least three years. She listened while Mitch gave her a blow-by-blow account of his day at the plant, including the clandestine meeting of the two trucks at the storage facility.

"This is the proof Bruno wants, Mitch. You're a genius," she said in awe. He'd uncovered things with such lightning speed, she could hardly take it in. At this rate he'd be gone out of her life in a flash. She sprang to her feet in turmoil. "Excuse me for a moment."

She hurried to the bathroom, not wanting him to see her tears. The realization had just started to sink in. She needed to get a grip. After washing her face and applying fresh lipstick, she started back to the kitchen, praying he wouldn't know all the reasons she was torn up inside.

Since last Monday she'd been living with the knowledge that someone in her family was stealing from the company. That was bad enough, but in a week's time something else had transformed her personal world, shaking her to the roots.

Mitch Garrett had happened to her. She was crazy about him!

Her pulse raced when she saw him at the end of the hall waiting for her. "I know this has come as a blow," he said with compassion, "particularly because we're getting closer to fingering the suspects spearheading this. Naturally it pains you to think anyone in your family could be this treacherous. If you'd prefer that I deal solely with Bruno from here on out, I'll understand."

No-o— Mitch hadn't fully understood why she was so upset. She didn't dare tell him the truth. How could she? She knew he liked her, but she couldn't be positive he was attracted to her romantically. He'd had an opportunity to kiss her in the kitchen, and it killed her that he'd let the moment go.

When she'd grasped his arms a little while ago, she wasn't sure if the tremor she'd felt was because he hadn't liked the contact. Or maybe he *had* liked it, but didn't feel he could act on his feelings while he was doing his job as a P.I.

"I want to see this through," she asserted, trying to present a calm exterior. "What's the next move?"

An unreadable expression crept over his features. "Tonight I'm headed for the office to go through the videos taken at the plant. One of the crew from the surveillance van is going to bring me the tape taken after I left today. Once I've viewed all of them, I'll have a much better idea of who's involved."

"What can I do to help?"

She heard him take a deep breath. "Nothing at the moment. I'll phone you in the morning and tell you what I've learned. We'll go from there." At the front door he paused and turned to her. "What would be the best time to call?"

"Any time," she replied, wishing he didn't have to go. "I'm always up early."

Heidi thought she glimpsed a flash of desire in his eyes, but if she was right, he didn't act on it. The next thing she knew he was out the door. When he'd driven away, she locked up and hurried to the kitchen, needing to do something to get rid of the ache that had attacked her body since his arrival.

The first thing she thought of doing was to place the food in plastic bags and put them in the freezer. Her father and Bruno would want to see the evidence. She flattened the donut sack and slipped it in her purse for safekeeping.

Unable to concentrate on the ten o'clock news, filled as always with terrible things that had happened to people, she turned it off and got ready for bed. She could just imagine the field day the media would have if bad news leaked about the Bauer company.

But even that stayed in the background of her mind because all her thoughts were centered on Mitch. One day soon he'd be gone for good. The pain hit with full force.

Heidi didn't need to put a name to the reason for the pain. She'd fallen in love, totally, gut-wrenchingly in love. She knew it the way you knew the sun was going to come up in the morning.

After a restless night, she showered and washed her hair. Whatever the day brought, she wanted to look her best in case she saw Mitch. No—there was no *in case* about it. She planned on seeing him before the day was out.

Once she was dressed, she fixed breakfast for her and Zack. Together they put his bike and helmet in her car before driving to her parents' home. While she was getting it out of the trunk, she heard her cell phone ring, but she couldn't get to it. She'd left it on the front seat.

"Here you go, honey. Wheel it up to the porch."

She closed the trunk and got back in the car, saw that the call she'd missed was Mitch's and had to phone him. "Mitch?"

"Good morning. You sound out of breath."

She was always out of breath around him. "I couldn't reach my phone in time. Sorry."

"Where are you?"

"In my parents' driveway."

"You haven't seen them yet?"

"No. Why?"

"There's something I want you to look at and help me make sense of."

Her heart thudded. "Where are you?"

"At my apartment."

"I'll ask my folks to watch Zack for a little while and I'll be right over."

"You're sure?"

"Positive. Dad's as anxious as Bruno to stop what's been going on. I should be there in about ten minutes."

"Pull into the carport and park behind my car. I'll leave the door open."

Her body pulsated with excitement. "See you soon." She hung up.

"Are you going to go to Mitch's apartment?" Zack asked. He must've overheard her when he'd come around her side to wait for her.

"Yes," she answered honestly, "but I won't be long."

"I want to come with you."

"You can't, honey. Your grandparents are waiting for you."

"But I want to see Mitch."

Don't we all. "Maybe later."

"How come you're so mean?"

"Zack Norris—" she used her parental tone "—that was not a nice thing to say to me."

"I'm sorry," he muttered. "But can we do something with Mitch later?"

"I don't know what his plans are. Look! There are Grandma and Grandpa on the porch waiting for you. Show them how well you can ride your bike."

MITCH DRANK COFFEE on his veranda while he waited for Heidi. The air was unusually muggy this morning. After a full week of blue skies, fast-moving clouds had started massing. There'd be a thunderstorm before long, the kind he loved.

After coming home from the office late, he'd lain awake afterward tortured by longings for Heidi that were growing stronger by the second. Once she'd touched him, grasped him the way she had, that was it.

Though she'd done it blindly in reaction to the news, his gut told him it was a move totally out of character for her. A watershed moment, as far as he was concerned. If she had any idea how much he'd wanted to devour that gorgeous mouth of hers last night—

"Mitch?"

At the sound of her voice, he turned and went back to the kitchen. His breath caught at the sight of her. She wore a sensational-looking sundress of a rich plum color she filled out to perfection. It had, short pleated sleeves. That color with her golden hair made a miraculous combination. She was bare-legged and wore bone-colored sandals. He groaned inwardly. A man could only take so much.

He set his empty cup on the counter. "You look beautiful." Even that was an understatement.

She came back with "You're nice, but it's the dress."

Mitch saw a pulse throbbing at the base of her throat. Did she really not know how she affected a man? Her bad marriage had done even more damage than he'd thought.

"I get so sick of wearing pants every day," she said next.

"If you wore that at my mostly male office, you'd start a stampede."

She blushed. "Hardly."

Oh, lady. If you only knew.

He reached for a stack of photos he'd printed out at the office. "Let's go out on the veranda. With the cloud cover, the temperature is actually pleasant."

"I noticed that driving over. I noticed something else, too. Your car has Michigan license plates."

"I have my reasons." He followed her out the sliding door, getting the benefit of the subtle lemon scent he associated with her. After they sat down, he put the photos in front of her. Mitch was so on fire for her, he had to force himself not to pick her up and carry her to the bedroom.

"I viewed the tapes last night and enlarged certain segments into eight-by-ten photos for you," he said. "According to the organizational chart you drew for me, Nadine Owens oversees the entire mix process."

"Yes. She's Frieda's granddaughter and runs the show in there. Bruno gave her that job when I was put in as head of human resources."

"That explains why she's the one who inserts the yellow stock cards with the numbers and destinations."

Heidi nodded. "The count is so important, Bruno prefers a family member to be entrusted with that responsibility."

"I need to know more about Nadine. What's she like?"

Heidi averted her eyes. "If you want to know the truth, she intimidates me."

"You?"

"Just a little. She's pretty perfect in everything she does. As long as I can remember, she's worked for the company and still manages to have a happy marriage."

One of the many things Mitch loved about Heidi was her honesty. The divorce had really brought her down. "How old is she?"

"I think she's thirty-nine, maybe forty."

"Does she have a big family?"

"Two children, one in high school, the other in college. She's as dependable as a Swiss clock. That's how Bruno describes her. Hale and hearty. It's the reason he put her in that position. Her work ethic is amazing, a model for everyone else. As far as I know, she's never taken a sick day."

Mitch winced at her comments, hating even more what he had to do. "Take a look at this first picture, caught by the camera in the flour storage room at 2:30 p.m. yesterday afternoon. Isn't that person Nadine who appears to be instructing two of the men to load the motorized cart with flour?"

Heidi studied it for a minute. "Yes. The mix room must be low on inventory, so she's having more flour sent in."

Mitch didn't respond. Instead he put another picture in front of her. "This picture was taken at the same time by the camera in the mix room. If you'll notice, the shelving is full of flour bags and everyone is busy."

He watched her study the picture and noticed how quiet she'd suddenly gone. She didn't move a muscle.

"Here's a third picture. We're back to the flour room. Twenty-five bags of flour have now been loaded. Nadine is inserting the yellow stock cards between the last two bags."

"But those are flour bags…."

"That's right." Mitch handed her another picture. "This is the mix room again. Two men are loading the sealed bags of mix on top of the flour bags already placed on the cart. Now study this series of pictures."

She took them from him.

"You see here? A flour bag has just been put in among the mix bags. Nadine is inserting another yellow card. If you'll notice, all the other employees in the area are doing their own jobs, probably unaware of what's going on. These next two pictures show Lucas arriving ten minutes later to count the load."

Heidi gasped, studying each picture over and over again. "I'm seeing it, but I can't believe it!"

"The next stack of pictures shows the same process starting again at 3:30 p.m. in the flour room with Nadine, and ending with Lucas counting the second load. Here's the final picture." He slid it on top of the others. "It was taken in the warehouse bay at 5:00 p.m. It shows two loaded carts sitting out at the loading dock waiting for Tuesday morning."

"Oh, Mitch…" Her voice sounded desolate. She eventually lifted her head and looked at him through wet blue pools. "To see it happening before your very eyes… Nadine—of all people."

She shot up from the table. "She holds such a position of trust it would never occur to Bruno—to *any* of us. I wonder how many people in the mix room have known what's been going on and turned a blind eye…."

Without hesitation he pulled her into his arms, wanting to comfort her. "Maybe not as many as you think. Maybe none if they trust her so completely," he whispered into her fragrant curls. "We know for certain now Nadine is party to the thefts. Since she arrives at the plant earlier than Jonas or Lucas, she's had access to keys. If they're not to blame, then it's possible she knows their computer passwords and deletes the emails that would give her activities away."

"Don't forget the truck drivers who make the secret drop-off in Draper," Heidi said against his shoulder.

"Let's hold out on blaming them until we know all the facts. I've got to do some more investigating to find out if she's at the center, or if she's carrying out someone else's orders." He also needed to talk to the woman who'd worked under Nadine before she'd been let go by the company.

Heidi's shoulders shook. "When Bruno sees this, I'm afraid he'll have another stroke."

Mitch drew her closer. She fit against his body as if she were made for him. "Your great-uncle comes from tough pioneer stock like his grandmother, otherwise he wouldn't have survived his first stroke, let alone hired Roman's firm to do a thorough job of getting at the truth."

"You're right." Her voice was wobbly.

Her vulnerability was too much for Mitch. He kissed her temple and cheek until he found her mouth. Her immediate response to him was like a miracle. They took small experimental tastes of each other's lips. It was the most delightful moment of his life holding this fabulous woman in his arms, sensing that her desire for him was there pulsating beneath the surface.

But it only lasted a moment. To his frustration she eased away from him before he was ready to let her go and wiped her eyes. "Sorry I got your shirt wet."

"I'm not complaining." He pressed one more kiss to her mouth. "What I'd like to do is finish my investigation and identify the people involved. Then we'll go to Bruno with all the facts and let him deal with it the way he sees fit. If I were to feed him the information in pieces, he'll brood and speculate."

Her gaze searched his. "You're very perceptive."

"You forget I've been in the bloodhound business one way or the other since joining the Marines. You learn to read people fast."

She rubbed her arms with her hands. "Did you notice anything else suspicious while you were working in the plant yesterday?"

"Not really. As for my crew, so far they haven't picked up anything from listening in on the conversations in the offices I bugged. Do you know if Nadine favored company expansion like her grandmother Frieda?"

"I've never heard her express an opinion. Even if she's wanted to work against Bruno's philosophy, I still can't fathom her using her position to steal from the company. How come she feels no loyalty to him or the family? I don't see how that's possible."

"It's my opinion you're not the only one who's felt intimidated by her. Otherwise someone ought to have come forward by now. But her clever scheme of embezzlement is about to come to an end." Mitch gathered up the photos and put them on the counter. He flicked her a glance. "How soon do you need to pick up Zack?"

"Actually I told my parents I'd meet them at the ranch. Mom wants to see how the float for the parade is coming. Dad said he'd take Zack for a short horseback ride."

Mitch cocked his head. "In that case, come snooping with me."

Her face brightened, the sign he was hoping for. "Where?"

"I want to retrace my steps from last evening and check something out. We shouldn't be gone more than a couple of hours."

"I want to see that pub in Alpine."

Mitch thought she might. "So you shall." He reached for her purse and handed it to her. "If you'll back your car out, I'll do the same, then you can park here and we'll go in mine."

She walked out ahead of him. Once in the carport they bumped into his neighbors. He couldn't wait to be alone with Heidi again and only nodded to the girls. When he helped her in the car and they drove down the street, she turned to him with a curious look in her eye. "I believe they were disappointed you left so fast."

He made a turn onto Foothill Drive. "Any disappointment they felt happened when they caught sight of the gorgeous woman coming out of my apartment. In the morning, no less," he drawled.

She chuckled. "You're terrible."

That was another thing he loved about her. She didn't take herself too seriously. "I have news. We males are all terrible when it comes to a good-looking female."

"College girls have the same problem where a hunky Marine is concerned. I wonder how many months they've been waiting for you to come outside and play."

Mitch broke into laughter.

"One thing is certain," she added.

"What's that?" He would never get tired of being with her. Those days of needing his own space had vanished.

"Your parents passed on some attractive genes to you," she said. "If they could see how you've turned out, they'd be overjoyed."

He felt another tug on his emotions. "What brought that on?" By now they were on the freeway.

"I don't know exactly. Since you told me about your past, I've thought a lot about it. I guess it's because I'm a mother. What if you took out an ad in some of the Florida newspapers showing a Garrett Fruit Company crate with a statement like *I'm the baby you put in this crate thirty-four years ago. If you want to meet me, notify the paper at this email address.* Something like that."

Astounded by her interest, he said, "It's a terrific idea, but I'm afraid the paper would receive thousands of emails from people claiming to be that person."

She eyed him speculatively. "If you asked the newspaper to forward them to you, I'd be happy to help you go through them. You never know what might happen, but if you don't like that idea, here's another one. Have you considered taking time off from all your work and doing your own investigation full-time to see if you can trace them? You know—physician, heal thyself?"

What a remarkable woman she was! Mitch gripped the steering wheel tighter. "When I was in the Marines, I used to think that when I'd earned enough money and didn't have to work, I'd do what you suggested. But before I was injured, I watched one of those televised documentaries where a woman who'd been abandoned at birth searched for her mother and finally found her."

"What happened?"

"It was a disaster on both sides and made me realize I'd better be careful what I ask for because I just might get it and not like it."

She studied him compassionately for a minute. "You'd rather they came looking for you?"

"In an ideal world," he admitted. "I'm afraid that's the child in me—just waiting for a dream to come true."

"We all have that child in us," she said in a faintly mournful voice.

The tone of their conversation had turned more serious.

"Were you terribly in love with your husband?"

He heard her sigh. "Whatever that means, at the age of twenty I thought I was. Then the oddest thing happened." She paused. "We got married and he changed, became someone else, someone angry and controlling. By the time Zack was born, my old feelings for him had died. Gary was eventually fired at work and from that point on his anger grew worse. I couldn't do anything right and filed for divorce. Such a relief."

Knowing the kind of principled woman Heidi was, he realized divorce was the very last option she would have considered. Their marriage had to have been unbearable. "How long were you married?"

"Four years."

"Well, I happen to know your son loves his mother with all his heart, so you're doing everything right in his eyes."

She laughed. "You didn't hear him this morning when he found out I was going to be with you. He said I was *mean* not to let him come. I told him I didn't know what your plans would be."

"Zack's a very special boy. When we've finished our business down south, how would you like for us to head north and pick him up? Depending on the weather, we might even drive to that amusement park I've seen from the highway."

"You mean Lagoon?"

"Yes. I've passed it several times, but haven't gone in because it's the kind of place to enjoy as a family."

She went quiet before looking at the sky. "By the time we reach the ranch, we'll probably be wiped out by rain, so it will be better not to mention it."

If she was trying to discourage him, it wasn't working. For days now the chemistry had been building. She wanted this day with him as much as he did—he could feel it. A fire had been licking through the veins of them both back at his apartment. Heat was building. Before long it would turn into a conflagration. His heart thudded at the thought of making love to her.

THE MAN DRIVING THE AUDI was dressed in gray trousers and an expensive-looking silk sport shirt in a charcoal color. When Heidi had been in his arms, she'd smelled the soap he'd used in the shower, and the scent still lingered in the car.

Inside and out, Mitch was close to perfect. She knew no one was perfect, but so far she couldn't find any fault in him. That was a pretty strong conclusion to reach when you'd only known someone six days!

Lost in thought, she didn't realize they'd come to the turnoff for Alpine until she heard a police siren and saw a car being pursued. "Uh-oh. Somebody was speeding."

"That's made the patrolman's day," Mitch said in a dry tone. "It'll help him make his quota to please his boss."

She turned her head toward him. "How many car chases have you been in?"

"A few, but when a felon is fleeing the scene of a crime, more times than not we're both on foot."

Everything he'd done in his life from the Marines to the federal marshals to his P.I. job revealed he preferred to live dangerously. The world needed men like him to keep other people safe, but a woman who cared for him might have a big problem with that. Was it the reason he'd never settled down with a wife? Because he knew she could never handle the risks he took?

Could you handle it, Heidi?

She'd already answered the question several days ago. She would hate watching him walk out the door wondering if it would be the last time she saw him alive. The sooner he left Salt Lake, the better for her and Zack.

While Mitch drove them into the business center, she trembled because the truth stared her in the face.

She was a pathetic mass of contradictions. If she thought it was better he moved back to Florida, then why had she dressed up this morning wanting him to notice?

You know why, Heidi. You want to keep him here for good.

"Here's the strip mall," he said. "The pub is in the center." As they passed slowly by, she was able to see the sign. *Homemade donuts and pizza.* "I'll drive around back. The pub won't be open for an hour, but someone has to be there setting things up. Let's see what we can find out."

There was a flash of lightning in the sky as they pulled into the alley where other cars were parked. Heidi saw a cell phone truck delivering boxes to the store near the other end. When Mitch pulled up to the back door of the pub and got out of the car, she resisted the urge to tell him to be careful. Though he knew what he was doing, he wasn't infallible. He had scars from his gunshot surgery to prove it.

A guy who looked to be in his twenties answered the knock. Wearing a T-shirt and jeans, he'd tied an apron around his waist. Heidi's heart hammered in apprehension while Mitch talked to him. The guy listened, then shook his head before shutting the door.

"What did you say to him?" she asked as he got back in the car. The wind was gusting. She could smell rain in the air.

He started the engine and drove them to the end of the alley. "I told him I was out here from Michigan looking for a friend named Mario. He was supposed to be working at a pub in Alpine with another friend named Eric. The guy said his name was Nick and he'd never heard of either guy. Does the name Nick mean anything to you, Heidi?"

"No."

"He said there was another place in Lehi called Ronny's Pub. Maybe Mario worked there."

She shook her head. "Your creativity blows me away. Did you see anything incriminating?"

His gaze met hers. "A storage room filled with Bauer bags. I could smell donuts cooking from another section. Now that I've seen evidence that the place is in full operation with stolen goods, there's just one more thing I want to check before we drive to the ranch to pick up Zack. We'll have to backtrack to Draper."

"To that storage place where you saw the bags being transferred?"

He nodded. "I want to see if it's just a rendezvous point, or if one of those guys is actually using a storage shed where they were doing the loading. Lon is tracing the license plate on the pickup and the two cars in the supermarket parking lot. I should be hearing from him today. In the meantime, maybe we'll get a break and find something that will give us another lead."

Once they were back on the freeway, he said, "Heidi, I'm not sure you're all right. I shouldn't have brought you with me."

"Bruno asked me to be his eyes and ears. I could cry buckets over what Nadine has done, but I needed to come. It's making everything real."

Mitch reached for her hand. At his touch she felt the contact arc through her. They sped north while the elements treated them to a fabulous display of forked lightning followed by thunder. But another kind of fireworks were going off inside her.

"The wind's so strong, it's buffeting your car."

"We're in for a downpour all right."

By the time they reached the Draper turnoff, the sky was black with clouds. "Ooh—it's getting close," she said.

"Does it make you nervous?"

"No. I love storms."

He gave her hand another squeeze before letting go. "So do I. We're almost there."

Sheet lightning lit up the entrance to the storage facility. She had no idea where they were going, but Mitch had little problem finding what he wanted with his own built-in radar.

"Here we are. Row K." He drove to the end of it and stopped. "This storm has sprung up at the perfect time. No one's here. I'm going to open a couple of these sheds and look around. You stay in the car."

"I want to look with you." She slid out her side and watched him use a tool to open the end shed. Inside were a dozen lawn mowers and snow blowers.

"That shed's no help." Mitch closed and locked it. Jagged lightning flickered overhead followed by a huge thunderclap that shook the ground, but he kept working and opened the next shed. Hail started to bounce everywhere, but she was hardly aware of it because her attention was suddenly focused on the black Mazda Miata parked inside.

More lightning illuminated everything. Before he shut the shed door, she caught sight of the custom-made Bellagio spinner tire rims on the older model sports car.

"Oh, no!"

"Get back in the car, Heidi." By now hail was slamming them hard. Mitch grabbed her around the shoulders and forced her into the passenger seat of the Audi. He shut the car door and ran around to get in behind the wheel, sealing them inside.

The hail was coming down now as if the heavens had emptied, covering the ground like snow. He leaned across and pulled her into him. "Don't be frightened. This'll be over in a few minutes."

A monsoonlike rain followed the hail, enveloping them in the deluge. Shocked senseless by her discovery, she lifted her head. "That's not why I cried out."

"What then?" he demanded anxiously. Heidi felt the warmth of his breath on her mouth.

"That Miata is my ex-husband's sports car!"

Chapter Seven

In the pounding noise of the rain, Mitch's teeth clenched so hard he almost cracked one. With lightning flashing, he could see that her complexion had lost color. He drew in a labored breath. "You couldn't possibly be mistaken?"

"No," she declared with complete conviction. "I'd know his Miata anywhere. It meant more to him than his own family. After we got married, we lived in an apartment. Our goal was to buy a house in two years' time using our savings for a substantial down payment.

"Our problems came about early because he wanted us to have joint savings and checking accounts. But my father advised me not to set things up that way. Gary accused me of being paranoid about money, but as the months went by I realized he was dipping into his savings to work on the car. By the end of our first year of marriage I was expecting Zack, so I asked Gary if he'd given up on the idea of a house.

"That's when he had a major meltdown. He told me point-blank he would never make enough money with his lowly warehouse job at the plant to match my salary. I reminded him he could move up if he finished college and went for his MBA. Or he could go out and look for the kind of job he truly wanted. The next thing I knew, he slammed the door behind him and left to buy those expensive special rims for his car."

Mitch saw her jaw harden. "I should have seen the signs of blind ambition in him, but hormones got in the way. It's clear love didn't motivate him to marry me. He wanted a shortcut to money. It's no wonder he was so upset when he couldn't get into my accounts. What I'm trying to understand is how he and Nadine grew close enough to join forces. All this time I thought he was in Oregon. This is the proof that Zack means absolutely *nothing* to him! I feel doubly savaged."

The hurt in her voice tore him up inside. "So do I," Mitch said, "but remember they've taken wrong paths of their own free will and aren't worthy to breathe the same air you do. I've had to deal with felons for a long time. Most of them have had something happen in their childhoods that a majority of psychiatrists refer to as a brain freeze."

"I've heard that theory, too."

"It's probably because they never bonded with anyone. If certain emotions like empathy and remorse—the kind you and I feel—get cut off, then behavior can grow more immoral over time."

She wiped her eyes. "That describes Gary. He resented having to live with his grandparents after his parents died in a boating accident." Her head jerked around. "But look at you—you never had a family to bond with, yet you're wonderful!"

Heidi, Heidi.

"So are you," he whispered, pulling her across his lap so that she half lay in his arms. "So wonderful and so beautiful, I don't have words. Forgive me, but I have to do this or I won't be able to function."

Her sweet mouth had lured him from day one. At his apartment her lips had teased him. But now that he was covering them with his own, he was lost in sensation after sensation. His heart leaped to realize their hunger was mutual. He found himself kissing her face and hair, her throat where a pulse was madly beating. Her hands on his chest took his breath away, enthralling him in a way he hadn't dared dream about.

"You're more beautiful to me than you can imagine," he whispered against the side of her neck. "Not just physically. I see the way you care for your son, the way you cherish those you love. You're fun and exciting and amazing and so many other things...."

"You're amazing, too, Mitch." She ran kisses along his jaw. "I never expected to meet someone like you when Bruno asked me to drive to the Lufka firm."

As Mitch half moaned her name in longing, a car honked loud and long behind them, causing her to sit up abruptly and move to her side of the Audi. She looked back. "What if that's Gary?" she cried in panic.

"Don't be frightened. It's an older man, but we're probably blocking his shed." The rain had turned to drizzle while they'd been entwined. You could see rivulets of floating hail.

"We'd better move."

Yup. The interruption was ill-timed, but he had no choice except to start the engine and head for the exit.

He knew in his gut Heidi was just as shaken by the passion that had flared between them. It had taken over conscious thought. If that driver hadn't come along...

On their way out to the highway he flicked her a glance. "Before we drive any farther, I want to be clear about something. I have no intention of asking your forgiveness for what happened back there."

"That's good, because I don't expect one," she confessed with her unfailing honesty. That's what he loved about her. That resilient spirit.

"I could blame it on the amazing dress you're wearing, but that wouldn't be the truth. You already know I've been intensely attracted to you from the moment you walked in my office. In all honesty, after we'd finished making our first batch of donuts, I wanted to drag you back to my cave by your incredible hair. Whether you believe me or not, I've never gotten involved with a client before. You're my first.

"Wait—I take that back. Once, when I was a federal marshal guarding a woman who'd been put in the witness protection program, we found ourselves attracted due to the time we'd had to spend together. Fortunately I got out before I jeopardized the case."

He heard her take a swift breath. "Then fortune is still with you."

"What do you mean?"

She stared at him. "Inside of a week you've all but solved this case for my great uncle without jeopardizing it, either. In a few more days you'll have tied up the loose ends and can head back to Florida.

"After watching you in action, I can't imagine this P.I. job holding a man like you for long, not with your skills and instincts." She sighed. "You're overqualified for the work of a private detective, Agent X12."

He grimaced. After getting into each other's arms, those thrilling feelings they'd both experienced had frightened her. *Damn Gary Norris for robbing her of her confidence.* But Mitch wouldn't allow her defenses to thwart him. This called for different tactics. You didn't rush a woman like Heidi.

"Let's not get ahead of ourselves. Those loose ends could take some time. If you feel you've got other things to do and can no longer help me, I understand."

"You know that's not what I said."

"Then you're not frightened of me?"

"Of *you?* No."

It was an answer of sorts. "For your information," he said, "this situation is new to me, too. But none of it matters as long as we have complete trust and are frank with each other." *As long as we stay together and explore what's going on here.*

"You really mean that?"

"Heidi—"

"Let's assume the shoe was on the other foot and after seeing each other for a week, I told you I was headed for my home across the country, still on a quest to locate my mother or father. It wouldn't be a vacation. I planned to return to a job I loved and had held for a long time." Her eyes blazed with fire. "Knowing those facts, how much of an investment would you make in me?"

Once her question had rung out in the car's interior, she reached for her phone and called her parents to find out their plans. When she hung up she said, "Because of the rain, they're already on their way back from the ranch with Zack. If you wouldn't mind, Mitch, I'd like to stop at your place and get my car. I need to talk to my dad about what we've found out and prepare him. He's going to take this hard and will blame himself for firing Gary."

"I don't think so. Your ex-husband took a left turn long before his blowup with your father, and your dad knows it." He reached for her hand. "And you need to stop taking on any more guilt for marrying him."

"Actually, I have stopped," she said before slowly removing her hand from his grasp.

Mitch hoped she meant it. After learning her ex-husband had been close to Salt Lake all along and had played a role in this crime against her family, naturally she would go straight to her dad to talk to him.

Maybe it was selfish of Mitch, but he wanted her to come to him, Mitch. Just the way Mitch wanted his father or mother to come to him?

You're out of your mind, Garrett.

They drove the rest of the way to his apartment in silence. At the entrance to the carport, she was out of his car before he could stop her. He saw the bleakness in her eyes when she leaned in to speak. "In light of what we've just learned, I want to thank you for the drive. But under the circumstances, that doesn't sound quite right, does it?" Her strength after being confronted by such adversity was a revelation to him.

"No," he murmured. "If you and Zack decide you'd like to come over here later, I have calls to make and am not going anyplace. Don't forget I promised him he could work out in my mini-gym."

She nodded. "I haven't forgotten. Neither has he."

On that note he watched her climb into her car, back out and drive off. After her taillights disappeared, he phoned Travis hoping he'd pick up. He needed to talk to one of his buddies or he was going to explode. To his chagrin, he got his voice mail.

"Travis? It's Mitch. When you've got a minute, call me. This is important."

After he let himself into the apartment, he made himself a cup of coffee. While he was draining it, his phone rang. He grabbed for it and checked the caller ID before clicking on. "What's up, Lon?"

"Lots."

"Go ahead."

"I checked the license plate on that pickup. It's registered to a Merrill Warburton, 81, at the home address you asked me to check."

Mitch sat down at the table so he could take notes. "The guy driving the pickup last night had to be in his late twenties, so it could be anyone living at that address with him."

"Right. I made a few phone calls to neighbors and found out Mr. Warburton passed away two and a half years ago. His only son, Cain Warburton, lives in Sacramento, California. His family is grown. He lets his oldest son, Levi Warburton, live there in Alpine and take care of his grandparents' place. This neighbor told me they've been trying to sell it, but no buyers yet. This Levi is single and has a single male living with him."

"You work miracles, Lon. It's all making sense."

"I got lucky and found a next-door neighbor who likes to talk. As for the Honda Accord in that supermarket parking lot, it's registered to a Jeremy Farnsworth, 27. The Ford Taurus is registered to a Noah Eldredge, 29. They both live in Alpine at different addresses."

"Great work. What about the truck driver who works for Bauer's?"

"Yeah, Matt Sayer. If he was on the wrong side of the law before working for them, then he never got caught until you got him on film."

"Things are starting to line up. What have you found on Gary Norris?"

"Well, there's no history of him living anywhere in Oregon in the last nine years. No warrants for his arrest. Zip. He still holds a current Utah driver's license."

Adrenaline charged Mitch's body. "At what address?"

When Lon told him, Mitch let out a low whistle. "That's his ex-wife's address. It means that when he renewed his license, he never changed his place of residence. It'll interest you to know Heidi and I found his sports car parked in one of those storage sheds in Draper this morning. What do you bet he lives at the Warburton house, where he can keep a low profile?"

"I'll drive down there and do some more investigating."

"As long as you're going, buy a meal in that pub in Alpine and see if you can get a visual on Norris. You've got picture ID. Once we can tie him to the pub, I'll have enough evidence to take to Bruno Bauer."

"I'm on my way."

"I owe you, Lon. This case is exceptionally important to me."

"Just doing my job."

"But no one does it like you do."

He'd barely hung up when Travis returned his call. He clicked on. "Thanks for getting back to me so fast."

"You sound upset. What's going on?"

"How long have you got?"

"You want me and Casey to drive in?"

Travis lived in the south end of the valley. "No, no. I just need to talk."

"This wouldn't have anything to do with Heidi Bauer, would it?"

"Who's been spreading rumors?"

"The usual suspects. Lisa noticed you *did* give your client and her son a private showing of the shop. Once she told Roman, that was it."

"Nothing's sacred."

"He comes from fine Russian stock and insists on knowing everything that goes on. He doesn't head a spy ring for nothing."

In spite of Mitch's turmoil, he smiled, but it didn't last. "Here's the problem. This morning Heidi and I found out her ex-husband is involved in this case up to his eyebrows." Mitch brought Travis up to speed.

"So he and this Nadine have been stealing the company blind. They're a real gutsy duo."

"Yup. I'm still reeling from the fact that he abandoned Heidi and Zack a long time ago. He gave up his parental rights after they divorced. Knowing he's indirectly back in her life in such an ugly way has made the case much more complicated for me on an emotional level because—"

"Because you're already emotionally involved with her up to *your* eyebrows," Travis finished the sentence.

"Afraid so. I want to be alone with her. You know what I mean? But I can't do anything about it while I'm in the middle of this case, so I want to offer support from a distance. How would you and Casey like to come to the parade with me on Monday morning? Zack is going to ride on the Bauer float and be dressed up like a pioneer child. I'd like to be there for him and Heidi. After learning of her ex-husband's betrayal, she needs to know I'm there for her."

"Casey and I would love to go to the parade with you. How old is Zack again?"

"Six."

"With Casey being seven, they'll have to meet. Count us in. I'll call Chaz and tell him to bring Lacey and Abby."

"You're reading my mind."

"I'll call him as soon as we get off the phone."

"Thanks, Travis."

"Stealing from her family's company on top of everything else is what I call the ultimate betrayal. I'm sorry for all concerned. Talk to you later, Mitch."

The empathy in Travis's tone stayed with him after they'd hung up. His friend had lived through something much worse after he'd learned his wife had been murdered. Mitch had suffered for him and Casey, too.

HEIDI GLANCED AT HER BOY. "Did you have fun with Grandma and Grandpa?" They'd just driven away from her parents' home.

"Yes, but it rained so we couldn't go riding. I'm glad we came back after lunch. Can we go over to Mitch's now? He said I could play with his gym stuff."

She knew Zack. He wouldn't let it go, so she made a decision. Better deal with this immediately or he'd drive her crazy for the rest of the day. "Tell you what. Here's my phone." She passed it back to him from the front seat. "Press two and Mitch should answer. Find out what his plans are." Heidi was afraid to let Mitch know how eager she was to be with him again.

"Goody." In a few seconds her son was talking to Mitch, who had him laughing. Their conversation went on for as long as it took to reach her house. "Okay. See ya. Hey, Mom? Mitch wants us to come over now. He rented a scary spy movie for us to watch after we work out."

That sounded like Mitch. He *was* pretty perfect. Ask her son. But the haunting thought that he was close to resuming his federal marshal job gripped her like a vise.

"All right. While you put your bike in the garage, I'll change clothes and we'll go." She retrieved her phone and opened the trunk to get out his bike.

"Do you *have* to change? He told me to hurry."

"It won't take me long." The dress she had on was a reminder of the way he'd looked at her before their mouths had fused in raw hunger. That memory would always live with her whether she removed it or not, but she would still feel better showing up at his apartment in jeans and a shirt.

Since seeing Gary's car, she'd had time to put the morning's discovery into perspective. It only under-lined the utter deadness of her feelings for her ex. They were so dead that when Mitch had cocooned her in his arms and had driven their kiss deeper, she'd been on fire for him. Forget the world. Forget the case Mitch had been hired to solve. Forget everything except Mitch's way of bringing out her deepest emotions.

Earlier Mitch had asked her if she'd been in love with her husband. Whatever feelings she'd had in those days, Gary had systematically killed them. She didn't know how empty she'd been until Mitch had come along, bringing her back to life.

Ten minutes later she and Zack entered his apartment. "Hi, Mitch! I brought my walkie-talkies."

"So I see." Mitch squeezed him on the shoulder. "I'm glad you remembered." He put them on the counter. "After we finish exercising, we'll have some fun. Go ahead and check out the equipment in the other room. I'll be right in."

"Thanks."

As Zack took off, Mitch's gaze swept over Heidi. She felt a quickening because by the look he was giving her, she might as well have been wearing the sundress. "Did you tell your parents what we've discovered?"

"I told them we have evidence that Nadine is one of the culprits. That came as a huge shock to them. I didn't say anything about Gary, because Zack was right there. We agreed to put off our talk until Monday night. It's going to be a big day and we don't want to ruin it for anyone or act like anything's wrong."

"I think that's the wisest course. It'll give me time tomorrow to check out some more leads."

She nodded. "After the parade, there'll be a big barbecue at the ranch for those in the family who want to go. The kids will play and then I'll take Zack home and put him to bed. My parents will come by then. Dad wants you there. Is that all right with you?"

"Of course. I plan to be at the parade, too, and get pictures of Zack. Where would be the best place to watch it?"

While Heidi waited for her heartbeat to slow down

after hearing that news, Zack called out from the other room. "Hey, Mitch, aren't you coming?"

"I'll be right there!"

"The parade starts at nine and ends at Liberty Park. If you get to the north end of the park early, you'll be able to find a parking spot. I'll be riding in the car with Karl, who's driving the float. Zack told me he's too nervous to ride on it unless I'm there, too. Karl's the one who ferries Bruno to work and back. We'll be the first float behind my father and the horse cavalcade."

Mitch's eyes gleamed. "I'll find you."

Mitch...

"While I'm playing with Zack, do me a favor and see if you can reach that female employee from the mix room who was fired a few months ago. Use my laptop to get into the files and find her phone number. If possible, get her to tell you what led up to her being fired. Use my phone so she won't be thrown off by your name." He put it on the table before striding off to join Zack.

With some trepidation, Heidi sat at the table against the wall to begin her task. They'd gone over that list before. Deena Larson had been let go in April. Since Heidi had been the one to recommend her for the job, it had come as a big surprise to learn she'd been fired after the first day. To Heidi's knowledge, nothing like that had ever happened before, but she supposed there was always a first time.

Deena and her husband had moved from Evanston, Wyoming, to Salt Lake, where her husband was looking for work. She'd worked as a pastry chef at a local bakery and came with a high recommendation from her former boss. Heidi had been impressed with her.

The file indicated that Lucas had done the firing, but there was no written explanation for it.

Curious in her own right, Heidi picked up Mitch's phone and called the first number listed. She reached Deena's voice mail, so she tried the second number. After three rings, a female voice answered, probably from her cell phone. "Hello?"

Heidi bit her lip before she said, "Hi. This is Heidi Norris. I'm the person from Human Resources at Bauer Donuts who recommended that you be hired in April. Do you remember me?"

There was a long period of quiet. "Yes. What do you want?"

At least she hadn't hung up on her. "This is an unofficial call. I've been going through some files and came across your name. When you were let go in April, I have to admit I was really surprised because you made a very favorable impression on me during our interview. Have you found another job yet?"

"Yes."

"I'm glad for that. Deena…would you be willing to tell me what happened? You'd only been working in the mix room a day. If you thought you'd been dismissed unfairly, I'd like to know about it."

"I guess from the man's point of view, it wasn't unfair. I *did* challenge him."

"Who? What do you mean?"

"It was the end of the shift. As I was leaving, one of the warehouse men—the name Lewis was on his tag— drove the motorized cart into the room. I saw some bags already on it. That surprised me, so I checked the tags. They were flour bags. I told him to take the bags back to the flour storage area."

"I would have told him the same thing," Heidi interjected.

"Well, he told me those bags were *supposed* to be there. But that didn't seem right since they were supposed to be loaded on the truck. I'm afraid we got in an argument, so I went to Mrs. Owens's office, but she wasn't there. The only thing to do was leave the plant and talk to her about it the next day.

"But I never got the chance. Later that evening, I received a call from Lucas Bauer, the warehouse manager. He told me that Lewis had been with Bauer's for four years and the company didn't tolerate interference or insubordination from its employees. They ran a smooth ship, so I was being let go with a week's pay."

At least they'd given her *some* compensation, but with hindsight Heidi realized Deena had walked into something criminal without knowing it.

"I knew what had happened to me wasn't right, but I didn't have time to fight it. I've learned from experience that if you get off on the wrong foot from the beginning, things don't normally go right. Our family needed money and I needed to find another job quick."

Deena was a nice, decent person. "I'm so sorry, Mrs. Larson. Thank you for being willing to talk to me. I appreciate it more than you know."

Heidi hung up, horrified by what had happened to the woman. She hadn't been wrong about Deena who was intelligent and bright and had tried to prevent what she'd thought had been a mistake. Heidi should have checked into the firing and gone to Bruno, but at the time she hadn't been a witness to the argument, and she'd still been lacking the necessary confidence to go up against Lucas in a "he said, she said" situation.

She jumped up from the table and hurried down the hall. As she peeked around the door her gaze fell on Zack who was lying on a bench doing a bench press with dumbbells. Mitch stood next to him, cheering him on. They both saw her at the same time.

"Look at me, Mom!"

"You're getting a real workout."

"I know."

Mitch chuckled. "We're both worn out. Let's stop for a while."

"Do I have to?"

"Yup. You don't want to strain your muscles."

"Okay."

While he was putting the dumbbells away, Mitch walked over and gave her a searching look. "Any luck?"

She nodded. "I'll tell you later."

"Hey sport," he called over his shoulder, "do you want to watch that spy movie? If your mom will fix the popcorn, I'll make us some wild berry punch. I always drink it after a workout."

"Yum. I'm thirsty."

"So am I."

In a few minutes they'd settled down in the living room with drinks and snacks. Zack got on the floor to watch the film. Once he was involved, she turned to Mitch. In a quiet voice she told him what she'd learned.

He reflected for a moment. "Since you've been in charge of Human Resources, how many people have you interviewed for jobs in the mix room besides Deena?"

"None. That group has been together a long time. Patsy Reardon was forced to give up her job and move to North Dakota to take care of her ailing mother. It was the first job to come available there in several years. Deena's background check was impeccable. When I met her, I thought she'd be a perfect fit."

Mitch's eyebrows lifted. "Too perfect. They had to get rid of her in order to stop her from upsetting a well-laid-out plan of embezzlement that had been functioning brilliantly for several months."

Zack suddenly got up from the floor and came to sit between them. Heidi knew why he'd moved. So did Mitch, whose lips twitched. Her son wanted them to be quiet and pay attention to the movie. As if he couldn't help himself, Mitch put his arm around him and gave him a squeeze. "You like this movie, sport?"

"Yeah. Don't you?"

Mitch burst into laughter. "Yes, but I have an idea. When it's over, let's drive up to the zoo. Since the rain, it's cooler out. We'll buy some hot dogs and walk around. Maybe the orangutans will put on a show."

"Hey—they're my favorite, too! They're funny, huh, Mom?"

"Hilarious."

"Their baby does all kinds of crazy stuff and gets in trouble."

Mitch's face broke out in a grin. "Have you seen him swing that tire around?"

"Yeah. He's strong for a baby."

"Maybe we ought to go to the zoo right now. When we've seen the animals we want, we can come back and finish watching the movie. Your mother and I promise to be quiet."

His blue eyes glowed. "I bet you can't." Her son was a riot.

"Bet we can." Mitch got in the last word.

Two hours later they returned to his apartment, still laughing from the orangutans' antics. The spider monkeys were pretty funny, too.

They freshened up, then went back to the living room, ready to watch the rest of the movie. Before Heidi could sit down, someone was leaving a message on Mitch's answering machine. It was in the kitchen, but loud enough to be heard.

"Now hear this, Mitch Garrett. Remember your old boss Lew Davies? How come I haven't heard from you lately? I hope you're winding up that case you've been working on, because I just received word that has made my day. Whitey Filmore's back in custody. It's time for you to come home. Call me as soon as you get this message."

Zack couldn't have comprehended all of it, but he'd figured out enough to stare at Mitch with haunted eyes. Heidi's heart had already plummeted a thousand feet.

"How soon do you have to go home, Mitch?"

"That's none of our business," Heidi advised her son. "Come on. Let's finish watching the movie."

"I don't want to."

Mitch hunkered down in front of him. "That guy Lew is an old friend of mine who was just clowning around, Zack. I'm not leaving Salt Lake yet. For one thing, you're going to be in the parade on Monday. You think I'd miss that?"

Zack's eyes were suspiciously bright. "You're really coming?"

"Would I lie to you?"

Heidi had to wait to hear her son whisper no.

"Can you say that a little louder please?" Mitch prodded him.

All of a sudden Zack smiled. Miracle of miracles.

"I've already arranged it with your mother."

When Zack looked to her for confirmation, she nodded. "He's going to be at Liberty Park."

"Yup," Mitch said. "I'll be there with my friends taking pictures of you in your pioneer costume. I'll be wearing a cowboy outfit with a white hat because I'm one of the good guys. You won't have any trouble spotting me. Now how about we finish watching the movie. The really good part is coming."

If there was a really good part, it passed by Heidi in a flash. The second the movie was over, she stood up. "We've got to go home now, Zack. Can you thank Mitch for a wonderful day?"

"But we haven't played with the walkie-talkies yet."

"Zack!"

With a penitent look he said, "Thanks for working out with me, Mitch."

"Thank *you*," Mitch answered. "It's a lot more fun when you have a buddy."

"Yeah."

Mitch flicked Heidi a glance. "I'll call you tomorrow evening when I'm through doing my research."

Zack looked up at him. "Do you have to work on Sunday?"

"This Sunday I do."

Heidi opened the front door. "Come on, Zack." She was afraid he was going to ask Mitch to go to Sunday school with them.

"Okay."

She knew how her son felt. Heidi didn't want to leave, either. Their host walked them out to her car and helped Zack inside. "Thanks again, Mitch." Without looking at him, she backed the car to the street.

On the short drive home she made a decision. Once Monday was over and Mitch had met with her father, she'd go back to work at headquarters on Tuesday and make certain there was no more togetherness. The message on Mitch's answering machine had been like a bucket of ice water thrown in her face. Zack had been hit by it, too.

But that was good. It had brought them both to the understanding that Mitch's days out west were numbered. Soon his cowboy hat would be nothing more than a souvenir.

Chapter Eight

"What do you think?" Mitch stood in front of the mirror at the Saddleman's Emporium wearing cowboy boots and a Western shirt with fringe.

"You look like you just walked off a Hollywood Western movie set," Chaz teased.

"Yeah?"

"Yeah. That shirt looks more authentic than the plaid one you tried on." He handed him the cowboy hat. "Now let's see the whole bit."

When Mitch put the hat on and pulled the rim lower, Chaz nodded. "It's an improvement over the marshal hat you left back in Florida. I think this one's a keeper." The subtle hint that Chaz wanted Mitch to stay on at Lufka's wasn't wasted on Mitch. "You'll be impossible for Zack to miss now."

"That's the idea."

Lew's phone message, escaping the way it did throughout his apartment at the worst possible moment yesterday, had caused definite repercussions. Particularly after Heidi had forced him to look at their situation without rose-colored glasses.

Heidi had gone all quiet. As for Zack... To his chagrin, Mitch could do nothing about anything until he'd finished the job for Bruno Bauer.

"Thanks for breaking away from your family to meet me for breakfast, Chaz."

"Lacey was glad to get rid of me for a while."

Mitch flashed him a knowing glance. "Liar. Marriage agrees with you."

"You're right. I'm so happy I go around in a daze."

"I've noticed," Mitch drawled.

He grabbed his T-shirt and shoes from the chair and walked over to the counter. He asked for a bag to put his things in and handed the clerk a credit card. Before he turned away, he said, "You wouldn't happen to have a white cowboy hat like mine to fit a six-year-old, would you?"

"Sure we do." She walked to the end of the store and produced one for him made to order.

"Zack's going to like this." He paid for it and put it in the bag. "Thank you."

He looked at Chaz. "Since I'm driving down to Alpine right now to do some more sniffing around, this outfit ought to fit right in with all the cowboys down there. Maybe I'll get lucky and see Gary Norris on the premises." He squinted. "That'll make my day. Lon didn't have any luck spotting him when he went down there to look around."

They walked out of the store to their cars. "Nevertheless, watch your back," Chaz said.

Mitch nodded. "I'll get to Liberty park early in the morning tomorrow and save us all a place."

"Abby's so excited, she's doing double butterfly loops around the condo because she can't wait."

"Neither can I," Mitch murmured.

After waving each other off, Mitch started his Audi and headed for the freeway. Today there was no sign of a storm. The sky was a hot blue overhead. His thoughts shot ahead. If he couldn't find Norris at the pub, he'd start checking out the three addresses.

Twenty-five minutes later he found parking along the street in front of the Alpine strip mall. It was twelve-thirty and already the place was bustling with moviegoers and shoppers. Sunday was a big day evidently. He got out of his car, noticing people going in and out of the pub. You could hear the music outside.

Mitch checked out a couple of other stores before walking in. He spotted Georgia waiting on a table. Just the person he wanted to talk to. A group of teenagers got up from one of the tables, so he took their place. Pretty soon she came over.

When she saw who it was, she flashed him an inviting smile. "I was hoping I'd see you in here again. You look hot in those duds."

"Thank you, ma'am. You're looking pretty fine yourself. When's your next break?"

"Not until two."

"Can't you take it now?"

"No. My boss would fire me."

"Maybe he'll make an exception if I ask him. Is he in the back?"

"Yes, but please don't bother him. I need this job."

He could see she meant it. "Okay. I don't want to get you in trouble. Then will you bring me a cup of coffee and a donut to go?"

"Sure thing." If a few minutes she was back with his order. "I'm off at six tonight."

"I'm afraid I won't be around then." He handed her a twenty-dollar bill. "Keep the change."

"Thanks. Next time your order is on me."

"I'll keep that in mind, sugar."

He walked back to the restroom area in order to take a look around. This was the second time he'd been in the pub. Three employees had been on duty both times. The strip mall hadn't been there long. In this good a location, the people who owned or leased these properties paid higher rent. Someone with money had to be funding this place.

He tipped his hat to Georgia before leaving the pub. Once back in his car, he drove to the end of the street, made a right, then turned right again into the alley. Most likely the cars he saw here belonged to employees. He spied an empty space near the pub's rear entrance and parked the Audi.

The nearby waste-disposal bin, probably shared by several of the stores, looked full to the brim. On a whim, Mitch got out to take a look. The Dumpster was filled with boxes. He peered inside as many as he could reach and hit the jackpot on the last box, which felt heavier than the others. When he opened it, he found a discarded container of Cramer cooking oil, the same brand Bauer's used in their outlets. If he dug deep, he'd probably find a lot more discards.

Mitch took a picture with his iPhone and hurried back to his car. After removing his hat, he called Lon.

"Hey, Mitch. Got something new for me?"

"Always. I need a couple of things. First, can you find out who either owns or leases the Drop In Family Pub in Alpine?" He gave him the address. "Secondly, the oil used to cook Bauer's donuts comes from a company called Cramer's in Stockton, California. If we could talk to someone there, they might tell you who does the ordering for the Drop In Pub. I know it's a Sunday, and Monday's a holiday, so you might not be able to find out anything until Tuesday."

"Oh, ye of little faith." Mitch smiled. "Where are you?"

"In Alpine doing surveillance."

"If you need backup, holler." They disconnected.

Mitch wanted a look at Georgia's boss and figured whoever it was would leave the pub at some point during the afternoon. Though Mitch was tempted to phone Heidi while he waited, he had nothing new to tell her about the case. Until he'd fingered everyone connected, he couldn't talk to her about future plans. Tomorrow they'd be together. For the moment his job was to sit here and wait for something to happen.

When ten minutes had gone by, he drank his coffee before it grew too cold to tolerate. No sooner had he finished it than he saw a tall man come out of the pub pushing a road bike out the door. He carried his cyclist's helmet. It was Gary Norris!

Mitch had seen his picture at Heidi's house when Zack had showed him his room.

Gotcha.

Mitch took a series of photos, then started up the car to follow him. Sure enough he pedaled to the Warburton home two miles away. When he dropped his bike in the front yard, Mitch got more photos of him hurrying up the porch steps into the house. No sign of the pickup truck.

The guy might be in there for half an hour or all day. It didn't matter to Mitch. He'd found what he'd been looking for and headed to Salt Lake. Norris didn't have enough money for a second car, but he didn't dare drive his Miata, which was too distinctive. Had he always ridden a bike? Had he cycled with Heidi early on in their marriage?

Before he drove himself crazy with questions, he phoned the guys doing surveillance in the van outside the plant in Woods Cross. "What's your day been like?" he asked when Phil picked up.

"Nothing's going on here. We listened in on the conversations until they left the plant last night, but we didn't pick up anything that sounds remotely suspect."

"Maybe Jonas and Lucas aren't involved. Today I got positive ID on Gary Norris. He's the manager at the Drop In Family Pub in Alpine. We have positive ID on Nadine Owens, who handles the switch. We know how the bags are being transferred to the pub. What I'm waiting for is that final piece of evidence to link them on paper. Lon's working on that for me as we speak."

"Anything else we can do?"

"I won't need you on surveillance any longer, but be available in case of an emergency. Thanks for a great job."

"You bet. See you at the office."

After he clicked off, he called Roman and left a voice message, giving him the most recent update on the case. "I'll need your help for a warrant to subpoena the phone records on Nadine Owens and Gary Norris.

"One more thing. Tomorrow morning the guys and I will be watching the parade at the north end of Liberty Park. Zack Norris is riding on the Bauer float. If you're interested, why don't you meet up with us? We're going to have a picnic right there. I'll give Lisa a call to see if she'd like to come, too. See you later."

Maybe Heidi would want to be with her family at the ranch barbecue after the parade. She'd said it was going to be a big affair, but she hadn't shared her actual plans with him. In case she tried to get out of being with him at the park, he would invite her and Zack to join him and the P.I. crowd and see what happened.

The second he got back to his apartment, he sat down on the end of the bed and pulled off his new cowboy boots. He hadn't done much walking in them, yet his feet were already sore. The boots would take some breaking in. That's what the salesclerk had told him and he believed her.

Needing to channel his energy into something physical, he changed into shorts and a T-shirt, then took off up Emigration Canyon on his bike, where he did his best thinking. The exercise was great for releasing tension and Mitch had tension by the bucketloads.

On top of everything else on his mind, he thought about Heidi's suggestion of placing a newspaper ad using the orange crate as a visual reminder. As an idea for locating his mother or father, it was brilliant. But he couldn't imagine anything coming of it.

What he *could* imagine was being with her tomorrow. All day.

And all night? Didn't he wish.

Mitch rode until dusk before returning home to make a certain phone call. Tonight he would have to be content with just hearing her voice.

"Do I HAVE TO WEAR THAT straw hat tomorrow? It looks stupid."

Heidi had put Zack to bed, but he was nowhere near ready to go to sleep. "It's part of your costume. How many pioneer boys do you think walked across the plains with Marine haircuts?"

"Maybe a whole bunch. Mitch says they're cooler."

These days Mitch was the authority on everything. "That's true, but Sylvia planned all the outfits. You don't want to disappoint her, do you?"

"It's itchy."

"Well, you can take it off and on. How's that?"

"I don't like hats."

If Heidi told him how cute he looked in it with those suspenders and plaid shirt, he'd hate it. "Let's not worry about that now. You need sleep so you'll feel good while you're riding on the float. It gets hot when you're standing up there waving."

"What if I get thirsty?"

"Sylvia has water bottles hidden for you."

"I might have to go to the bathroom."

"Just hold it."

"Did you ever have to go to the bathroom when you rode on the float?"

"I don't remember, but I'm sure you'll be too excited to even think about it."

"Do you think Mitch will really come?"

"Has he ever let you down?"

"No."

"There's your answer, then. Good night, honey."

"Hey, the phone's ringing. I bet it's Mitch. He said he'd call."

She'd been waiting to hear from him for hours and

suspected that was why Zack hadn't been able to settle down yet. "Hello?" she said after clicking on, hoping she didn't sound as breathless as she felt.

It was Mitch.

"Hi! Have I phoned too late to speak to Zack?"

"No. He's right here. Just a minute."

Zack had already scrambled out of bed and took the cell phone from her. "Hi, Mitch." They talked for a few minutes. Mostly her son laughed. "Yeah. I have to wear suspenders." More giggles. "Okay. See you in the morning." He handed her the phone. "Mitch wants to talk to you."

"Now will you go to bed?"

Zack nodded and climbed under the covers. She turned off his light and walked down the hall to the living room. "Thanks for remembering to call. I think he'll fall asleep now."

"At his age, I would have been awake all night waiting for the big event. It isn't every day a boy gets to ride on a float in front of thousands of people."

"You're right." She sat down on the couch, tucking one leg underneath her. "Did you learn anything new today?"

"Yes, but I'd prefer we talk about that tomorrow night when we meet with your father. I'm afraid I'm as excited as Zack for morning to come. When I see your float, I'll follow it to the drop-off point. Will it say 'Bauer' on it?"

She smiled secretly. "No, but I promise it will stand out. You won't be able to miss it."

"Especially not with your son stealing the show. It's getting late and I know you have to be up early, so I'll

let you go. I'm looking forward to tomorrow, Heidi."
His voice came across deep and husky.

"Zack and I are, too. Good night."

She hung up, sensing Mitch had learned something
new about Gary he thought would upset her. What he
didn't know was that there was nothing about her ex-
husband's activities that would surprise her now. Gary
had failed to be a father to their son. His relinquish-
ing his God-given fatherly right of his own free will
was the most grievous part of all he'd done in showing
himself to be a miserable human being.

In truth Heidi was glad Mitch hadn't wanted to get
into anything unpleasant tonight. She had no idea what
the future held, but he made her happy beyond com-
prehension. Since time was running out, tomorrow
she would grab hold of that happiness while she still
could.

Sleep came while she was reliving those moments
in his arms during the storm. She'd experienced much
more than a physical rush and wanted desperately to
explore what was going on between them.

When her alarm clock went off the next morning
at seven, she leaped out of bed so excited to see Mitch
that time passed by in a blur before they were on their
way to the city center in Heidi's mom's car.

"There's our float!" Zack called.

Heidi's mom pulled her car to a stop on a side street
feeding into South Temple near the start of the parade.
"I think it's the most beautiful one we've ever had."

"Sylvia's committee really outdid themselves this
year." Her Bauer cousin and her husband, Daniel,
lived on the ranch and took care of the horses. Sylvia
loved the Pioneer Holiday. Heidi got out of the car with

Zack, wearing her jeans and a new blue shirt. "Thanks for the ride, Mom. We'll see you and dad at Liberty Park." Her father had driven into town early.

"Have fun, darling," the older woman said to Zack.

"I will. Bye, Grandma."

Zack was excited to join the other Bauer children, most of whom were already being placed on the float. Sylvia had said there would be sixteen of them from the ages of six to twelve. This was the first year Zack could ride on it. Their costumes looked authentic. From a distance Heidi had a hard time believing they weren't pioneer children from 1847.

Heidi gave her son a kiss. "Remember I'll be right inside the float. Keep waving and smiling. Here's your hat. I love you."

"I love you, too."

Sylvia's husband, Daniel, took Zack in hand and swung him up on the float. While he was being shown where to stand, Heidi slipped through the side of the float into the truck. Karl flashed her a grin from behind the wheel. "I know it's hot in here. The temperature is already ninety degrees and climbing. As soon as Daniel gives us the all clear, I'll turn on the AC."

"You wouldn't think we'd need it with only thirteen city blocks to cover. I'm just thankful we're the first float in the parade." They couldn't get to Liberty Park soon enough for her. When she thought of seeing Mitch, her pulse raced and she felt feverish. Yesterday was the first day they hadn't been together in a week. It had been the longest day of her life.

"Amen to that. I've brought some water bottles if you get thirsty."

"Thanks, Karl. I'll probably need at least one. Is Bruno coming?"

"No. Bernice wouldn't let him. They're going to watch it on TV."

"I think that's a good idea. Oh—I can hear the band. It looks like we're ready to roll. I set the DVR to record so Zack and I can watch the whole thing later."

"Sally didn't want to bring the baby out in this heat, so she's home recording it for me and the kids. Well, here we go." He turned on the engine and before long cool air flowed through the cab. They both looked at each other and said, "Heaven."

WHILE MITCH'S BUDDIES were busy staking out their corner of the park, he sat in one of their camp chairs to watch the beginning of the parade on his iPhone. The television studio producing the broadcast had set up their booth on State Street. He wanted to hear the commentary.

After the welcoming speech and announcement of dignitaries attending the celebration, the parade MC took over. Mitch listened and watched intently.

"Ladies and gentlemen, we are delighted to present the Grand Marshal of this year's Days of '47 Parade. Give a big hand to Erntz J. Bauer, riding his favorite horse, Prince. He's one of our prominent heads of industry in the Beehive State. Bauer Donuts is a name synonymous with the building up of the West. The first Bauer came into the Valley from Austria in 1892 and immediately contributed to the welfare of our community. The Bauer name is renowned through-out the western states."

Heidi had shown Mitch pictures of her father last week. The blue-eyed man was probably six feet tall. He looked trim as he sat astride his chestnut performing maneuvers with great expertise while he carried the Utah flag. He wore a black cowboy hat and fringed Western jacket. Though he was in his sixties, he still had thick, blond curly hair. Heidi had definitely inherited his coloring.

Odd as it was, emotion clogged Mitch's throat. The man being honored was Heidi's father and Zack's grandfather. What a heritage they'd all come from. He watched him lead the sheriff's mounted posse. It was followed by the University of Utah marching band. Then he caught sight of the first float.

"The beautiful float passing in front of the stands with the huge papier-mâché donuts has been made by the Bauer Donuts Company. Their motto is 'Press forward and onward.' Sixteen Bauer children, descendants of Saska Bauer, who started Bauer's, are dressed in pioneer clothing re-created from their family's pioneer photographs. The giant donut dominating the float has a field shaped like the Austrian eidelweiss flower. It's filled with freshly picked Eidelweiss grown on the Bauer ranch. The first thing Saska did after she started growing potatoes was put in a garden to grow eidelweiss in this land of the everlasting hills."

The camera zoomed in on the children. Mitch's eyes smarted when he saw Zack waving to the crowd with a hat in his hand. Heidi's son had gotten to him from the moment they were introduced. Right now that cute little guy was so precious to him he realized that what he felt for the boy was love. Pure love.

After clearing his throat, he got up and walked

around. Chaz flicked him a glance. "Are you all right?" he asked.

"Yes. I'm just anxious for Zack's float to show up here at the park so I can wave to him." Seeing him on his iPhone wasn't the same thing.

"I couldn't tell. Have a drink on me." He handed him a cola from one of the coolers packed with ice. They both drained their cans.

"Thanks. That tasted good. I think I'll walk down a couple of blocks to keep an eye out for them."

"I'll tell the others."

Mitch took off, working his way through the crowds of people lining the street along Ninth South. Many of them had slept along the parade route overnight. The usual clowns and police on motorcycles moved back and forth along the route. Finally he heard the band in the distance. After a few more minutes it passed, followed by Heidi's father, then the posse. But by now Mitch's eyes were focused on the float containing the two people he cared about most in the world. He started taking pictures.

"Hey, Zack, over here!"

Zack's head jerked around. When he saw Mitch, his flushed face broke out in a huge smile. "Mitch!" He waved his hat.

As the float moved toward the park, Mitch wended his way through the crowd to stay in full view of Zack. The procession passed by the area where Mitch and his friends had stationed themselves. It soon entered the park and the float came to a stop.

"Hey, sport!" Mitch crossed to the boy and reached for him. Without hesitation Zack lunged for him. When he felt those arms wind tightly around the neck, he was too moved by emotion to talk for a minute. He finally got the words out. "You were great up there."

"Thanks."

"Was it fun?"

"Yeah, but it's sure hot." Zack leaned back to look at him. "I wish I had a cowboy hat like yours. I could pick you out of everybody."

"That's why I wore it. Let's find your mom."

"She's underneath the float."

Children and parents were clustered around the chaotic scene, but there was only one woman in the world he knew with golden curls like Heidi's. "Mom, over here!" Zack had seen her, too.

Her gaze swung in their direction. Mitch felt a sudden stillness when she emerged from the crowd looking gorgeous in hip-hugging jeans and a summery, pale blue top that matched the color of her eyes. She moved toward them and reached for her son.

"I'm so proud of you, honey." As she hugged him, her eyes lifted to Mitch. They sparkled like precious gems. "Howdy, pardner," she said in a low voice. "Didn't know you'd rolled into Dodge." Zack laughed. "How long do you figure on stayin'?"

Mitch wasn't sure if it was a loaded question or not. He tipped his hat back. "Well, now, ma'am," he said with a smile. "That all depends on how happy you are to see me."

"We're *very* happy to see you, aren't we, Zack?"

"Yeah!"

Her answer would have to do for now. "In that case, stroll on over and meet my friends. I'll rustle you up something to eat and drink."

Though the guys were careful, Mitch saw them

glance at Heidi and give him a silent nod of approval. Once introductions were made and everyone was enjoying the picnic, Abby wanted to play with Zack's straw hat. While she put it on over her bouncy red curls, Mitch produced the hat he'd bought for Zack and plopped it on his head.

"You got me one, too?"

"Yeah. It keeps the sun out of your eyes."

"Thanks!" Buying him a hat was such a small thing, but Mitch was honored with another bone-cracking hug. "I love it!"

Heidi's eyes thanked him.

Travis and his son, Casey, had both come to the parade wearing black cowboy hats. Roman got out his camera. "This calls for a group picture, *Comrades*." He loved to use his Russian jargon on them from time to time. "We need a couple of pictures for posterity."

The wives plied Heidi with questions about her pioneer ancestry. Everyone studiously avoided any mention of the reason she'd come to the Lufka firm in the first place. The guys got up a game of Frisbee, but Mitch failed to catch it several times because his attention wasn't what it should have been.

As perfect and beautiful a picture as all this might appear, it had a lot wrong with it. Today the Bauers had been featured prominently in the pioneer festivities, yet one of their own was stealing from them.

This morning Zack had ridden on the Bauer float. Any parent would be bursting with pride to call him son, yet Zack's father was down in Alpine, getting away with more crimes against the company and his own flesh and blood.

The call from Lew Davies before Mitch had left his

apartment earlier had robbed him of some of the joy in showing off Heidi and Zack to his boss and good friends. *I really need you here, Mitch. We're all missing you and want you back ASAP. How soon can I expect you?*

An hour ago the beauty of this picture-perfect day had been further marred by the question Heidi had posed in a little different way. *How long do you figure on stayin'?*

The answer to that question was still up in the air.

When the Frisbee game had finished, Roman made an announcement. "Brittany and I want everyone to come swimming at our house." His invitation was met with cheers.

Zack walked back to the group with Mitch. "We didn't bring our suits."

"That's no problem. Ask your mother if she wants to go. If she says yes, I'll drive you home in my car and we'll get our stuff."

"Goody!" He ran on ahead to talk to Heidi. She was busy helping with the cleanup. In a second he darted back to Mitch. "She said it sounds like a lot of fun."

It *did* sound like a lot of fun, but he knew she had weightier things on her mind. Today was a case of the sweet. Tonight the bitter would come when they had to sit down with her father and Bruno.

Chapter Nine

"Zack's already asleep, Mom. He passed out early, thank goodness."

"After the day you've had, I'm not surprised."

"Thanks for staying with him."

"I'm glad to do it. Bernice thinks it's better you meet at Bruno's."

"I agree, but I don't know how long we'll be there."

"It doesn't matter. Stop worrying."

Heidi kissed her cheek. "I can hear a car in the driveway. That'll be Mitch."

"One of these days I'd like to meet the man you've fallen in love with."

Her mother's blunt comment caught her off guard. "There's a reason I'd rather you didn't. I may be in love, but he's not in love with me, Mom. It's called lust. The two are different animals."

"Heidi Bauer!" She couldn't remember the last time her mother had been upset with her. But her mother hadn't heard his answer when Heidi had asked him how long he was going to be in town. You don't build dreams on *That all depends on how happy you are to see me.*

What kind of answer was that? She felt certain

he would never pull himself away from Florida—
especially as he had hope of finding his mother there.
Besides, it was clear a job as a P.I. couldn't possibly
compete with the excitement and danger of a job as a
federal marshal. He hadn't even been worried about
Whitey Filmore. The fact that the guy was back behind
bars didn't matter to him one way or the other.

"I learned my lesson with Gary," Heidi said now.
"Facts are facts. Mitch's home is in Florida and he'll
be going back there now that this case is coming to an
end. Gotta run."

She hurried out of the house. "Sorry to keep you
waiting," she said to Mitch, who was just striding up
the walk. Heidi had never seen him in a sport coat and
trousers before. The tan color suited him. Everything
suited him. He looked sensational.

"Was Zack being difficult?" After he helped her
into the car, she gave him the directions to Bruno's
house.

"No. He went right to bed. That cowboy hat is hanging on his bedpost. Thanks for spoiling him. Every
little boy needs special attention once in a while. Since
we're alone, I'd like to tell you how much I enjoyed
your friends today. They're wonderful, all of them."

"They thought you and Zack were pretty terrific,
too."

"That's nice to hear. Brittney and Lacey told stories about how their husbands figured out within a
week who'd been stalking them. I told them you'd only
been on my case a week and had already solved it. You
men are an awesome group. I really can't thank you
enough. You'll hear my family's gratitude when we
meet at Bruno's."

His mouth thinned. "Have you finished?"

She blinked. "What do you mean?"

"I mean it sounds like you're ready to send me off into the wild blue yonder."

"I don't know what you're talking about."

"Oh, yes, you do." He suddenly pulled the car to the side of the road and turned off the engine. "Maybe it's because we haven't had a moment's privacy until this minute." She didn't have time to take another breath before he reached over and pulled her into his arms as he'd done during the storm.

"I don't know about you, but being in that pool with you this afternoon unable to do what I wanted with you has sent me out of my mind. I need this before we do anything else." He covered her mouth with refined ferocity, giving her one deep kiss after another.

At first she clung to him, wanting him with every cell in her body. But as their passion escalated, she feared that if she kept on responding the way she wanted to, she'd surrender her heart and suffer the consequences when he was gone.

"Mitch." She moaned his name, fighting the natural urges of her body.

"Don't pull away from me," he cried softly when he realized she wasn't giving as freely as before. "I've been living for this all day."

"The feeling will pass. It *has* to." Heidi sat up with difficulty and moved to her side of the car. "This isn't going to work, snatching a moment here and another one there. Have you forgotten we're due at my great-uncle's house in five minutes?"

"I've forgotten nothing and am damning the fact that we have to go anywhere or do anything else tonight except be in each other's arms. Do you have any idea how much I want you? Don't make this any harder than it is on us. I can't take it."

"Do you doubt that I want you any less? You think this isn't as hard on me?" Even though they weren't touching, she felt the shudder that passed through his body. "I'm going to be frank with you about something I didn't mention yesterday.

"I haven't been with any man since Gary. My failed marriage has made me nervous to get close to a man again. I was never this on fire for him and it scares me. If I didn't have a child, maybe I'd be willing to give into my desire until it burned itself out, but for Zack's sake I won't act that irresponsibly. Surely you understand!"

"I'm trying."

She threw her head back. "In case you didn't notice, we're now five minutes late."

After a tension-filled silence he started the car and drove them the rest of the way without talking. She'd taken the risk of angering him. He was definitely upset. But it was better than allowing things to get too far out of control.

Her dad's car was parked in front of the two-car garage of Bruno's home. Mitch pulled alongside it and killed the engine. She got out because she didn't want him to come around and help her. There'd be too great a chance of their arms or hips brushing. One look from his dark eyes could set her off and she'd succumb to the needs throbbing inside of her.

Bernice must have seen them drive up and held the door for them.

"Hi, Bernice." Heidi gave her a hug. "I'd like you

to meet Mitchell Garrett of the Roman Lufka Private Investigators firm. The best P.I. firm west of the Mississippi."

"That's what I've heard. How do you do, Mitchell. It's a pleasure." After they shook hands she said, "Your dad's in the study with Bruno. Go on in."

Briefcase in hand, Mitch followed Heidi down the hall to the study. Bruno, in a wheelchair that had been rolled in front of the big oak desk, was dressed in a smart-looking business suit. Her father, also wearing a dark blue suit, was deep in conversation with him, sitting forward with his hands clasped between his knees.

When Heidi walked in, he stood up and hugged her hard. She noticed Mitch shake hands with Bruno and introduce himself.

"You were awesome out there today, Dad."

Mitch joined her and nodded. "Watching you put your horse through the paces was a sight I won't forget." He shook her father's hand. "I'm honored to meet both of you gentlemen."

"Thank you very much. Seeing so many little Bauers on the float was a double thrill for me."

"Can you believe Zack made it through the whole thing?" Heidi interjected. "The children were amazing out in that heat."

"Of course they were," Bruno said. "Bernice and I watched the entire thing on television." He squeezed his wife's hand. She'd pulled up a chair next to him. "I was so proud I could hardly see the screen for the tears."

Heidi hurried over to kiss his cheek.

"Please—" Bernice gestured "—both of you sit down on the love seat."

When they'd done so, Mitch's dark brown eyes took in everyone. "I have to say this family has impressive roots. When Heidi accompanied me out to the plant so I could see the layout, she told me about your ancestor Saska Bauer. She was obviously a superwoman in a literal sense."

Bruno nodded. "Indeed she was and our Adelheide is just like her." Heat swept into Heidi's cheeks. "See that picture on the wall?" Heidi had noticed Mitch looking at it. "They're the spitting image of each other at Heidi's age now and they have the same brains."

"I'm convinced Zack inherited them, too." Mitch smiled. "He's smart as a whip."

"Speaking of intelligence, Heidi tells me you're brilliant at what you do. What about your roots, Mr. Garrett? You have a Germanic/French last name dating back to the seventh century."

Heidi shifted nervously on the seat. Bruno was the genealogist of the family, but this was one problem he couldn't solve and now wasn't the time to discuss it.

"I was abandoned as a baby, Mr. Bauer," Mitch explained, "in a church. I was in an orange crate that said Garrett Fruit Company. I have no idea of my ancestry."

All three of them studied him for a long moment before Bruno said, "Whatever your background, you must have genius in you or Adelheide would have told me we needed to find some other P.I."

Bernice nodded. "That's true."

Mitch darted Heidi a glance. "I'm flattered. Thank you for your faith in me."

Her heart thudded in her chest. "You're welcome."

"We understand you have news for us."

"Yes, Mr. Bauer. I think the best way to start is to let you sift through these pictures while I explain. I made two sets." He reached into his briefcase.

"I'll hand them out," Heidi offered and gave them each a pile. Bernice looked on with Bruno.

"This first set was taken at the plant by the cameras I installed on the day of the fire inspection. As you can see, Nadine Owens is the one setting things up to steal the bags during the afternoon shift."

"Nadine?" Both Bruno and Bernice said her name in a shocked cry.

Heidi exchanged a knowing glance with her father.

"The next set of pictures shows the stolen bags of flour and mix being taken off the truck and loaded into a pickup truck in Draper. More pictures reveal the pickup truck delivering the bags to the Drop In Family Pub in Alpine. If you'll notice the sign, it says homemade pizza and donuts.

"In the last set of pictures you'll see a familiar face coming out of the rear of the pub. It's the manager carrying a cyclist's helmet. You'll recognize Heidi's ex-husband, Gary Norris."

Bruno shook his head. "I don't believe what I'm seeing."

"I believe it about Gary," her normally temperate father declared with undisguised anger. "He was supposed to have gone back to Oregon."

"Mitch found out he never went there," Heidi told her father. "He lives in Alpine and is still driving his Mazda Miata." She reached into her purse and pulled out the plastic bags containing pizza and donuts she'd put in the freezer. "Mitch went into the pub and bought samples of the food, all made with Bauer flour and mix." She handed them around so everyone could examine the goods.

"Pizza?" Bernice sounded incredulous.

Heidi hunched her shoulders. "Who would have dreamed?"

"All this time I've thought it had to be Jonas or Lucas," Bruno muttered.

"Maybe they're involved," Mitch said. "I'm waiting for evidence from one of my crew about the person or persons who either own or lease that property in Alpine. It could be a third party, either family or not, who put up money to get the business started.

"By morning I'll have the pertinent information, but tonight you have enough evidence here to talk over how you want to proceed. Before I report for work in the warehouse tomorrow so no one suspects anything, I'll turn in my notes and film to Roman Lufka. When you're ready, he'll be happy to advise you about contacting the police."

Heidi's dad got up and walked over to shake Mitch's hand. "You've done us an invaluable service for which we can never repay you. The Lufka firm enjoys a stellar reputation. Now we know why." Bruno nodded in agreement.

"Thank you," Mitch said, "but don't forget you asked Heidi to assist me." She felt his burning glance on her. "She was brilliant in laying the groundwork for me in a clear, precise way. Anything I needed to know and she was right there with the answers. This case couldn't have moved as fast without her expertise. She really does know the Bauer Donut Company inside and out."

Bruno, still nodding, said in a voice choked with tears, "I knew it."

Stop, Mitch.

"When my boss told me I was going to love this case," Mitch went on, "it was because our firm can't live without coffee and Bauer SweetSpuds to keep us going. Can you imagine my joy when Heidi trained me how to make the donuts I've been consuming ever since I arrived in Salt Lake? I thought I'd died and gone to heaven."

While the men chuckled, Bernice's teary face broke out in a wobbly smile.

"Though I'm sorry my bloodhound services," Mitch added, "may have brought you untold grief, I have to confess that this case has been a pleasure I'll never forget."

Now Mitch was giving his goodbye speech. Heidi couldn't bear it. "Bruno? Is there any reason I shouldn't go back to work in the morning?"

"None at all."

Good. She turned to her father. "How soon are you leaving?"

"Now. It's late. Bruno and Bernice should be getting to bed and I have to pick up your mother."

"That's right," Bruno said. "We've all had a long day and need our sleep. I'll talk to you first thing in the morning, Ernst."

"Then I'll ride home with you, Dad." She turned to Mitch. "Bruno's right. It has been a long day and work starts early in the morning. Thanks again for driving me over here."

"Thank *you* for making my job not feel like a job."

She could still taste his searing kisses on her mouth and throat. "Good night, everyone. I'll see myself out."

Heidi watched him pick up his briefcase and leave the study on those long, hard-muscled legs. Tonight she was feeling so vulnerable, she needed the buffer her father provided in order not to chase after Mitch and show him what he truly meant to her.

MITCH'S CELL PHONE RANG while he was taking his break in the lunchroom at the plant in Woods Cross. He'd wanted to see if he could pick up any additional information while he ate with the employees. So far no luck.

He checked caller ID, wanting it to be Heidi, but knowing in his gut it wasn't. He'd spent a sleepless night because of her and was feeling like he'd been kicked unconscious and was just coming to.

"Lon?"

"I've got news. Nadine Bauer Owens is the only signer of the year's lease with Thackery Enterprises on the Drop In Family Pub property, dated January 3 of this year."

"The connection is complete, then. I've a hunch she and Gary have kept this between them."

"It appears that way. One more thing. The order for Cramer cooking oil comes from G. Norris, manager of the Drop In Family Pub."

"There's nobody who gets the job done as fast and as thoroughly as you, Lon. Turn in your research to Roman and expect a big bonus in your next paycheck. As of now, you're off the case and deserve a vacation."

"I could use one of those. It's always great working

with you, Mitch. I hope the rumor's not true about you heading back to Florida."

"We'll see. My work isn't quite through here."

"In case you didn't know, you'd really be missed if you left."

A lump lodged in his throat. "The feeling's mutual. Talk to you later."

He rang off before phoning Heidi's father and Bruno with the news about Nadine signing the lease. They'd already talked to Roman and would add this last vital piece of information to the rest. A meeting had been planned at the end of the day in Bruno's office. Mitch and Heidi were requested to meet with them and the police detective assigned to the case.

Gratified to know Heidi would be there, Mitch finished the afternoon shift at the plant. His last one. He was conscious of the fact that tomorrow there wouldn't be any more stolen bags of potato flour going out with the stolen bags of mix. A major shake-up in the Bauer family was about to occur.

But it couldn't be as big as the one happening to Mitch. Tonight after the meeting, he wouldn't let her escape him.

THE SECOND HEIDI GOT OFF the phone with her father, she phoned her sister-in-law. The news that Nadine had signed the lease for Gary put the proverbial final nail in the coffin.

"Sharon? I just found out Bruno has called a meeting in his office in a few minutes and I have to be there. Since it's almost time to pick Zack up from school, would you mind taking him home with your children? I'm sorry to do this to you, but it can't be helped. I promise I'll return the favor."

"I'll be happy to. Tim will be thrilled."

"Thanks. You're the greatest."

Heidi had worn a khaki skirt and a white top to work with her white sandals. She'd wanted to look good for her first day back at work in a week. Now that she would be seeing Mitch in a while, she was doubly grateful she'd taken the trouble. After this meeting, his work would be officially over. She wanted his last impression of her to be a good one before he left for Tallahassee.

She'd cried herself sick during the night and had awakened with puffy, bloodshot eyes. With cold water and concealing makeup, she'd managed to remove some of the sleepless signs. Once she'd made a trip to the ladies' room to brush her hair and add a fresh coat of lipstick, she climbed the stairs to the next floor and entered Bruno's suite.

Her dad met her with a hug, then introduced her to Detective Danvers of the Salt Lake City Police Department. "Honey, Mitch ought to be here any minute. Meanwhile, the detective wants you to tell him about your conversation with Deena Larson, the woman who'd been fired from her job after one day."

While Heidi told him the essence of her phone call with Deena, Mitch entered in the office dressed in a leaf-green polo shirt and khakis. He'd just come from the warehouse. Her body trembled every time she saw him. He flicked her a glance she couldn't read before being introduced to the detective.

Bruno cleared his throat. "If everyone will sit down, we'll let the detective explain what's going to happen."

"Thank you, Mr. Bauer. This evening several officers will arrest Nadine Owens at her home and take her downtown. At the same time, another set of officers who've made arrangements with the Utah County Police Department, will take Gary Norris into custody from his place of residence in Alpine and bring him to Salt Lake. Their pub operation will be closed down.

"Both will be put in jail. They'll be apprised of their rights and a public defender will be provided for them if they don't hire their own. Those of you who wish to talk to them will able to do so in the morning prior to their arraignment. At the time the judge hears their pleas, he'll set bail and name the date for a jury trial. Do any of you have questions?"

Heidi didn't. The reasons for what the criminals had done would come out in the trial. She had no desire to see or talk to Gary. She couldn't feel anything for him. Her heart was too shattered by the knowledge that she would be losing Mitch.

If there were another woman, she could fight for him. At least that's what she told herself. But how could she fight against his need to find his mother or father? It was a need he'd had from childhood. Maybe now he would take advantage of his free time to hunt for—

"Thank you, Detective Danvers," Bruno said, cutting off her thoughts. "This action is harsh, but Ernst and I have talked it over and feel it's necessary. Once we know they've been arrested, we'll phone each family member and tell them what has happened before they hear it on the ten o'clock news."

The old man teared up. "There's no doubt our family will be in mourning for a long time. Nadine is one of our own. Gary was once a part of us. I want to believe each family member will have charity in his heart for two souls who lost their way. We'll have to show increased love to Nadine's family. It's never too late for her or Gary to repent and make a fresh start.

"As for Lucas, he's been at the head of quality control and clearly not doing his job. He'll be reprimanded and put on probation. I'll also be having a talk with Jonas, who's in charge of the warehouse. His love for Lucas has made him less vigilant."

Heidi loved Bruno, who'd carried the mantle for so long. Without conscious thought she got out of her chair and ran over to hug him. "It's the right thing to do." Tears trickled down her cheeks. "I love you for your kindness and your convictions. Never *ever* change."

He wept against her arm. In another second her father joined them. Over his shoulder she saw the pain in Mitch's eyes before he slipped out of the room.

"Excuse me," she whispered.

After grabbing her purse, she ran after him. He moved like the wind. She didn't catch up to him until he'd reached his car in the parking lot. "Mitch!" At the sound of her voice he wheeled around with such a bleak expression on his face, she was shaken. "Why did you leave so fast?"

"My work is done and this is time for family."

Acutely aware he didn't have one, she said, "Agreed. I haven't seen Zack since early morning. I'm just on my way to pick him up at Sharon's. Will you meet us at my house? He'll want to say goodbye to you. I thought we'd order pizza and watch something silly on television that will make my son giggle. I—I need to hear his laughter...." Her voice faltered.

She could hear his mind working. "You're worried what you're going to have to tell him about his father one day."

"No," she answered with conviction. "I'm sure he'll handle it. Tonight I'm craving some happiness with my precious boy. We'd both enjoy your company. You've become a great friend." She stressed the word.

Mitch's mouth thinned to a white line.

"Do you have another commitment?" She remembered the haunted look in his eyes and wished she could take it away. "I don't care how professional you are. Knowing you were catching family and former family of mine in the act, I'm aware you haven't survived the experience completely unscathed."

His chest rose and fell with enough force for her to notice. "A dose of Zack would be a surefire antidote for the downside of my job." He hadn't denied it. "What can I bring?"

Her relief was exquisite. "How about your favorite ice cream?"

"Done."

"I should be home in a half hour. I'll hurry."

By the time she'd reached her car, he'd left the parking lot. She didn't regret inviting him to the house. If she'd had a secret agenda, it was so he could see Zack a final time and part company with him in a way her son would be able to handle. She'd said her farewells last night after wrenching her mouth from his.

When Heidi had been at the park after the parade, Brittany had mentioned how gloomy Roman had become because Mitch was leaving for Florida. The firm was losing a great friend, as well as a P.I. To his consternation, Roman couldn't stop Mitch from reporting back to his federal marshal's job, not now that his arm and shoulder had healed.

"Gloomy" might describe Roman. Heidi had another one for herself. Gutted. But she refused to get any more morose about it and sped home, anticipating their final evening together. When she drew up in front of Sharon's, she saw Zack and Tim playing teams against Rich with some water guns you launched from the shoulder. Her brother was big on anything that got you wet.

"Zack," she called to him. "Put your gun on the porch and come and get in the car. Don't forget your backpack and thank your uncle." She waved to her brother.

On the drive home, she eyed Zack through the rearview mirror. "That looked fun."

"Mitch would make it a lot funner."

She heaved a troubled sigh. "You mean 'more' fun. Zack, I missed you today. Did your friend Jacob go to the parade?"

"No. He said his dad hates them." Heidi tried not to smile. "Can we watch it again on the DVR? I want to see myself."

Her smile turned into a chuckle. "Oh, Zack. What would I do without you?"

"I don't know."

This time she burst into tearful laughter, probably because she was feeling almost hysterical.

"Hey, Mom, there's Mitch! I want to get out."

The blood pounded in her ears. "Not until we've parked the car."

The second she stopped, her son jumped down and hurried over to the handsome man pulling things out of his Audi. A grinning Zack rocked on his heels, a definite sign of joy beyond measure.

"Guess what? Mitch brought bubblegum ice cream and pizza with Canadian bacon from the Pizza Oven!" He was chattering a mile a minute as Heidi let them in the front door. The two males walked through to the kitchen with Mitch making comments here and there.

Heidi got as far as the hallway, then stopped because it came to her that if anyone were looking on, they'd think Zack and Mitch were father and son. Not because of their coloring, but because of the obvious bond between them. Something like the way Tim and Rich were.

Earlier at the office, when she'd seen Mitch standing outside the circle while Bruno wept, she'd sensed his aloneness. When the Bauer children got together with their fathers, how many times had she observed Zack standing off and *alone?* Heidi's was the only divorce in the family. Zack was the only child who showed up without a daddy. All the other children had one and functioned within those special spheres.

Tonight Zack and Mitch were relating within a sphere created by their own enjoyment of each other. Neither was standing outside looking in. This time they were the ones inside the bubble that wasn't visible to the naked eye.

Heidi watched and suffered new agony. Zack would be absolutely crushed when Mitch went away. It would take months for him to get over the feelings of loss. Not every man Heidi might meet in the future would accept Zack or appreciate his wonderful qualities the way Mitch did.

The unique man in her kitchen had grown up without real parents and so showed a special sensitivity around her son. He seemed to know instinctively how to make Zack feel good about himself. Would it bother Mitch to have to say goodbye to the little boy who worshipped the ground he walked on?

Would he miss *her?*

She watched Zack race down the hall to his bedroom. The next thing she knew he'd raced back to the kitchen, oblivious to Heidi. He'd put on the cowboy hat Mitch had given him and was carrying his walkie-talkies. Instead of water guns, they were going to play spy. Zack was in heaven.

Heidi groaned inwardly when she considered the void that would be left when Mitch was gone.

Chapter Ten

"It's past your bedtime, Zack. You've got school in the morning." Heidi gathered the cards to the Apples to Apples junior game the three of them had been playing on the kitchen table and put them in the box.

"Can't we play it again?" She heard the quiver in his voice. The moment she'd been dreading had come. With Mitch making everything exciting, the evening had been magical.

"I'm sorry, honey. Will you say good-night and thank him for dinner?"

Zack fastened soulful blue eyes on their guest. "Will you come to my school program on Friday at two o'clock?"

His question ignored hers and was so unexpected, a quiet gasp escaped Heidi's lips. She saw a flicker in the dark brown depths of Mitch's eyes and knew it had caught him off guard, too.

"You're in a program?"

He nodded. "Cuz it's the end of the year and we always do a big show for the moms and dads."

Adrenaline forced Heidi up from the table. "Honey, Mitch won't be able to come."

Tears filled Zack's eyes. "Are you going to Florida?"

"You know he is," she rushed to remind him. "Come on."

"Don't you like it here?"

A grim expression had crossed over Mitch's features. "Very much."

"Zack, it's his home, just like Salt Lake is ours. He had a job, but he got injured, so he came to Utah to have an operation. Now that he's better, he has to go back. His friends are there." *Family he's searching for.* She picked up her son because it was clear he wasn't about to move from the table.

"Casey said you're a federal marshal and got shot in the shoulder by an escaped prisoner," Zack said. "He said you almost died like his mom."

Oh, no.

When she'd seen the boys playing and talking together at the park, she'd had no idea what their conversation was about. Since yesterday Zack had been carrying this burden around without saying anything. Her gaze flew to Mitch for help. She saw a white ring of pain around his mouth.

"Will you show me?" Zack asked.

"You want to see my scar?" Mitch had asked the question, but he was still looking at Heidi. Though he was prepared to show Zack his scar, he wanted her permission and would do nothing if she didn't give it.

Heidi thought she'd loved Mitch before this moment, but that emotion couldn't touch the love she felt for him now. Since Zack already knew the truth, there was be no point in hiding anything from him. Mitch knew it and she knew it, so she gave him a nod.

"It's not a pretty sight, sport, but you're man enough to take it, right?"

"Right."

Mitch, darling... He always knew the right thing to say.

She watched in wonder as Mitch removed his polo shirt. When they'd gone swimming at Roman's, he'd worn a T-shirt the whole time, claiming he didn't want a sunburn.

In one of her fanciful moments early last week when they were getting ready to ride their bikes, she'd thought he looked godlike in the sun. Being so close she could see the dusting of hair on his well-defined chest, he resembled a Hellenic statue come to life in her kitchen.

But Zack was much more interested in the scar. "Wow! It's big!"

It was. Mitch would have suffered so horribly she couldn't bear it.

"Yup. There's a lot of it."

"Does it still hurt?" His anxious tone was so touching she wanted to cry.

"Nope. There's no feeling in the scar tissue. The great news is, my arm can move just like it did before." He made a circle to prove it.

Heidi managed to hold back her tears. "You really were blessed."

"Don't I know it," he whispered before putting his shirt back on.

"Now that you're better, you can be a federal marshal here," Zack reasoned. "Casey's father said so."

Mitch reached for Zack and carried him into the living room. Heidi followed them. They sat down on the couch with Zack on his lap. "What else did Casey tell you?"

"That you're a P.I. like the rest of them. He told me those walkie-talkies came from the shop at your office. I found out his dad used to be a Texas Ranger, and Chaz was a Navy SEAL."

Mitch's face broke out in a tender smile. "So you've discovered all our secrets. You make a great spy."

"Yup. Just like you. How come you don't stay here? Don't you like your friends?"

Mitch rubbed a hand over the top of Zack's head. "They're the greatest, but there's someone I'm looking for. I have to go back to Florida if I'm going to find them."

Heidi couldn't let this conversation go on without Mitch giving her son one piece of information Casey couldn't have known about or shared.

"Zack," she said, "have you noticed Mitch hasn't talked about his family?"

Her son blinked. "No." She saw alarm creep into his face. "Did something…bad happen to them? You know, like what happened to Casey's mom?"

When she saw lines darken Mitch's face she said, "Will you listen very carefully while he explains and not interrupt?"

Zack looked as surprised as the man holding him, but he nodded.

She stared at Mitch. "You need to tell Zack about the orange crate and go from there. It'll help him understand." Her son was facing a terrible few months ahead of him without Mitch, but Heidi was convinced that if he knew the truth, it might make the parting from his hero more bearable.

For the next few minutes Heidi was treated once again to Mitch's incredible story, only this time he had a captive audience in Zack. True to his word, her son didn't say a word. Even when Mitch had finished, silence filled the room.

Suddenly he slid off Mitch's lap and looked up at him. "My dad didn't want me," he said as one lone tear trickled down his flushed cheek. "But maybe if you find yours, he'll want you."

Mitch leaned forward and kissed Zack's forehead before putting his hands on his shoulders. "When I was your age, I assumed I wasn't wanted. It took years for me to realize that if the people who were my parents didn't have the money or other family members to help take care of me, that didn't necessarily mean they didn't want me. Maybe they were in bad health and couldn't. Do you know what I think?"

"What?" Zack's voice cracked.

"I think they left me at the church because they knew there would be kind people there who would look after me better than they could. Maybe your father felt he couldn't be the kind of dad you needed and he knew your mother would be the greatest mom in the whole world for you. Right?"

Zack nodded.

"I've never met a better mom than yours."

Heidi lowered her head, afraid she was going to break down in a puddle of tears.

"I hope you find yours, Mitch."

She heard Mitch breathe in sharply as Zack walked out of the room. Heartbroken for her son, she started to follow, but Mitch caught her from behind and pulled her against his chest.

"Let him be for a little while," he whispered against the side of her neck. He buried his face in her curls. "As long as everything is out in the open, let it percolate in him for a few minutes. I've been where he is now, both emotionally and physically. He needs time to process what's been going on. So do I."

Mitch spun her around, cupping her face in his hands. His dark eyes penetrated to her soul. "I'm leaving for Florida on the first flight out in the morning, but I couldn't go without kissing you goodbye."

Heidi moaned as he covered her mouth with his own. It wasn't like his other kisses. This one was like a brand, sending scorching heat through her body. When he finally relinquished her mouth and walked out the front door, she wanted to die, but she couldn't do that. She had a little boy to live for and cherish.

Her phone rang. She saw that it was Rich. He would have heard the news about the arrests from their father, but her thoughts were so far removed from anything except her love for Mitch and her son, she only had one need at the moment.

She flew down the hall to Zack's bedroom and wrapped her arms around him so they could comfort each other through the long hours of the night.

A YEAR HAD PASSED SINCE Mitch had entered the church in Tallahassee where he'd been left as a baby. He found out from the secretary that the parish had a new priest. She showed Mitch into his office.

"Father Bouchard?"

The slim, middle-aged priest made a welcoming gesture. "Come in, my son." He spoke with a faint French accent.

"Thank you for seeing me without any notice. My name is Mitchell Garrett. I just flew in from Salt Lake City, Utah, and came straight here."

"Please, sit down. What can I do for you?"

"Thirty-four years ago someone brought me to this church in an orange crate and left me here."

"Oh, yes." He touched his fingers together. "I remember Father Antoine telling me something about that. You're the Garrett boy who's been looking for your parents all these years. Aren't you in law enforcement?"

"Yes. I'm a federal marshal, but I got injured and had to take time off. I've been away, but now I'm back and came here first to see if you have any news for me. The secretary told me to talk to you."

He removed his glasses and rubbed the bridge of his nose. "Obviously if you'd found them, you wouldn't be here."

"No."

The priest sat back in his chair. "I would love to be of assistance."

"I'm sure you would. Everyone who knows my situation has gone out of their way to help me, but after all this time, it seems hopeless. Maybe I've been going about this the wrong way. If you have any suggestions, I'd appreciate them."

"Tell me a little about yourself first. Do you have a wife and children?"

Mitch got a suffocating feeling in his chest. "No."

"Were you ever married?"

"No."

"Why not?"

Mitch took a fortifying breath. "I'm not sure what the answer to that is anymore."

"Shall I tell you? It's because you've been marking time all these years, waiting for your life to happen. What a tragedy! You know how I know this? Because I was abandoned, too, and recognize the signs."

The priest's admission took him by surprise.

"You've allowed yourself to wallow in a land of unanswered questions while there's a whole world outside waiting to embrace you. But you've been afraid. You think you have to know who your people are before you can get onboard."

For the first time in his life, Mitch was hearing someone describe his inner struggle from the inside out.

"You came to this church for help. All I can give you is a piece of advice someone gave me. It changed my life. Do you want to hear it?"

"Yes."

"Leave your parents' whereabouts to God. He knows where they are, but *you* don't need to know. They've done their job. They gave you life. *Your* job is to live it fully. One day in the hereafter you'll meet them. They'll want to hear what you did with your life. Can you imagine how sad they'll be if they thought you spent your entire time looking for them?

"By an extraordinary circumstance, I came to America on the *QE2*. Pure luxury. I remember during the crossing how I thought about all the thousands and thousands of souls who'd come here years earlier by ship under miserable circumstances. Many of them were orphans, or had lost loved ones and were striking out for new shores."

A vision of the words on the Bauer float swam before Mitch's eyes. *Press Forward and Onward.*

"They didn't stay back pitying themselves and their lives," the priest continued. "They arrived here and made new lives. It was during that crossing I had my epiphany and I determined that I would embrace life to the fullest from that point on. I urge you to do the same."

The priest made so much sense, emotion had closed off Mitch's throat. He shot to his feet, breathless with new energy.

Startled, the priest stood up. "Have I been of help?"

"You have no idea," Mitch said in a thick voice. "Bless you."

With time running short—if he were going to get back to Salt Lake in time for Zack's program—he left the church and hailed a taxi. Twenty minutes later he entered the government building that housed the federal marshals' office. Lew Davies almost fell out of his chair when he saw him walk in.

"Mitchell Garrett, as I live and breathe. You look like a totally different man since the last time I saw you." He got out of his chair and came around to give Mitch a hug. "Talk about a sight for sore eyes…."

"It's good to see you, too."

"Damn it, Mitch. I've been waiting for your call. Why didn't you tell me you were coming today? I would have arranged a big bash for you."

Mitch had missed his old boss. "That's why I didn't want you to know."

Lew sensed something was different. He stared at him, trying to read between the lines. "You've changed. Sit down and tell me what's going on."

"So much has happened I hardly know where to start. To put it simply, I'm in love with this fabulous woman, and if she and her son will have me, we're going to get married."

He was rewarded with another hug. "That's the best news I ever heard! When's the wedding, and how soon is she moving out here?"

This was the hard part. "Lew…"

"Uh-oh. Don't tell me. You're going to live there and be a P.I. for the rest of your life."

Mitch nodded. "I don't have a family here. She has a terrific family there and I want to belong to it. I'll be flying back tomorrow night."

"Boy, when you move fast, no one can catch you."

Mitch studied his old friend. "You know I'll never forget my time with the agency. You've been the greatest boss in the world. In fact, I owe you more than you'll ever know. If it weren't for you trying to protect me, I would never have been sent to Salt Lake and I would never have met Heidi."

"Heidi, is it?" Lew smiled.

"Heidi's short for Adelheide. It's Austrian. She's so beautiful, Lew. And she's got a son named Zack any father would pray for."

"I'm going to have to meet them."

"I've got photos. If she says yes, you and Ina will be getting a wedding invitation."

"Is there any doubt your sweetheart will say yes?"

Mitch closed his eyes for a minute. "I haven't told her I love her yet."

A sound of exasperation escaped Lew. "For being the best federal marshal this office has ever seen, it's a different story when it comes to your love life. I've got to meet the woman who's finally brought down the legendary Mitch Garrett."

He patted Mitch on the back, then told him to sit. "You've got a ton of paperwork to fill out before you leave the department forever. I'll tell Nancy to get it ready. Then I want to see those photos."

At one-thirty on Friday afternoon, Heidi went to the school to peek in on Zack. After she checked to see that he was all right, she planned to grab a spot on the front row of the auditorium for her and her parents. But the second he saw her in the doorway of his first-grade classroom, Zack got up from his desk and ran over to her, teary-eyed.

A few mothers were helping the kids put on their costumes. Heidi assumed the white togas and fake laurel-leaf wreaths were meant to convey victory through excellence. His had slipped down over one eyebrow.

"I don't want to be in the program."

She put the wreath back in place. "I know you don't, but you have to." Life had to go on without Mitch, even if they were barely hanging on. Not one word from him, not even for Zack.

Mitch would never be intentionally cruel. It wasn't in him. But it was evident he felt that no more contact was the best way to handle their parting. Her mind recognized he'd done the right thing, but emotionally she was shattered and knew Zack was, too.

"I've got a stomachache."

Heidi believed him. This time she understood the reason. All the other kids had two parents who came to these programs. For the most part Zack had been handling his daddyless world pretty well. Then Mitch had come along. In a week he'd formed an attachment that gave him a taste of how great it would be to have the tough Marine around all the time. But Mitch was no longer available.

She could have told Zack how lucky he was that his grandfather Bauer would be coming. She could point out that there were kids whose grandfathers couldn't or wouldn't be in the audience. But even though he loved her father very much, it wasn't the same.

"I'll be right up front." He didn't like her to kiss him when the other kids were around. All she could do was squeeze his hand. "See you in a minute." As she walked away, the image of a forlorn little Julius Caesar stayed with her all the way to the auditorium.

The gym was filling up fast. She beat another family to the only seats remaining on the front row—at the end. Heidi had no idea where Zack would be sitting on the stage, but at least she'd be close. All of the grades, K-6, would be in the program, so there was a huge crowd. Pretty soon her parents appeared. They sat down next to her just before the principal called everyone to order.

"How's he doing?" her mom whispered.

"I don't know. We'll see if he makes it onstage."

Both her parents knew how crushed Zack was because Mitch had left. She loved them for offering their moral support, not only to him, but to her. There were families in the audience who knew of Gary's involvement in the embezzlement scheme. It had been in the news for several days now. Heidi had done everything to shield Zack.

Besides the fear that he might pick up on it, she

had an even greater worry. For the next three weeks, Zack was going to be out of school. She'd taken time off from work to be with him. A happy Zack would be one thing, but he was depressed. To prevent him from falling into a pattern of not wanting to play with anybody, she'd decided they were going on vacation.

First thing in the morning they were driving to Nebraska to visit Evy and see the new baby. The distraction would be good for him, and he'd be forced to interact with his cousins.

"I want to welcome mommies and daddies and grandparents and great-grandparents and everyone else to our school program," the school principal announced. "We're very proud of our children and their accomplishments. Our first class to come on stage will be the morning and afternoon kindergarten."

The teacher at the piano started playing. Heidi watched the kids with crowns march in, but didn't remember anything else. Her stomach had been upset all day waiting for Zack's part in the program. She was tired of fighting him and exhausted from crying into her pillow half the night.

Her dad nudged her in the ribs. "Zack's class is coming in."

She strained to find him. "I can't see him." Her anxiety increased.

"He's probably the last one," Ernst said.

Or maybe he'd decided to stay in the classroom. In about one second she would slip out and look for him. Being that she was on the end of the row made it easier for her. But someone else had just put a chair next to hers and sat down, blocking her exit.

Surprised, she turned to say excuse me, then almost fainted when she saw who it was. *"Mitch!"*

It couldn't be—

"Sorry I got here at the last second," he whispered. "My flight out of Atlanta was delayed." He grasped her hand, sending shock waves through her body.

She'd never known his dark eyes to be this alive, as if he were the keeper of some marvelous secret. Whatever the reason he was back in Salt Lake, the thrill of seeing the flesh-and-blood man made her giddy.

"Here he comes!" her mother exclaimed.

Heidi tore her eyes from Mitch's in order to find Zack and let him know they were there. He was third from the end on the other side of the stage. He walked with a solemn gait. She knew he was hating every minute of it.

Mitch leaned closer, brushing her ear with his lips. How she was breathing at all was a mystery to her. "He looks as if he's pondering the great speech he has to make before the Senate." It was so true, she had to fight not to burst out laughing. All she could do was squeeze his hand harder.

The children came forward in small groups to say a line. When it was Zack's turn, he and two other children stepped forward. Heidi's heart almost stopped beating when he looked in her direction and saw who was sitting next to her. It caused him to pause for a second before he remembered to say his part. After he got it out, his face lit up like someone had flipped on a switch.

Mitch gave him a thumbs-up.

Pretty soon his class had to file out to make room for the second-graders. Zack waved to the four of them before he disappeared behind the curtain. While the audience clapped, Mitch and her parents acknowledged each other and shook hands across Heidi, who sat there dazed.

When he sat back he felt for her hand again and tucked it under his arm. The proprietorial gesture sent fingers of delight up her arm. She glanced at his profile. "There's going to be a party in his class once this is over."

"You have no idea how much I've been looking forward to this."

Really?

Heidi was filled with questions, but now wasn't the time to ask them. It was enough he'd come to see Zack perform. It was a gesture more important to Zack than possibly even Heidi knew. These children were her son's peers. Now he had Mitch to champion him in front of them.

The rest of the program passed in a blur. She had no desire other than to absorb the reality of him. He'd come dressed in a stone-gray summer suit and tie. With his dark blond hair and rock-hard jaw, Heidi found him outrageously handsome. She rejoiced in being with him.

After the last group had performed, Mitch ushered her out of the gym and down the hall to Zack's room. While her parents went ahead of them, he kept a possessive hand at the small of her back, as if he needed to maintain constant contact. Heidi loved this sense of belonging. She'd never known a feeling like it.

They found Zack in a lineup in front of the room with the other children getting his picture taken in his costume. He was too restless to stand still. The second it was over, her parents were there to hug him. Heidi took her turn next, whether or not he liked her hugging him in front of the other kids.

"You did a great job today, honey. I'm very proud of you."

"Thanks," he said, but his eyes had focused on Mitch.

A lot of the children and parents were staring at the attractive man who let go of Heidi long enough to give him a hug. "You were awesome, sport."

Zack's face beamed. "You *came!* How come?"

"Because you asked me and because I wanted to." He helped him off with his costume. The teacher was gathering them.

"Did you go to Florida?"

That's what Heidi wanted to know.

"Yes, but I had to come back to clear up some unfinished business, and I wouldn't have missed your program."

"Oh."

Heidi's parents sent her a silence message of concern before they gravitated to the table for cookies and punch.

"Do you want to see my collage?" Zack said.

"I want to see everything," Mitch answered. "Lead the way."

It was at the other end of the room on the wall. Heidi noticed Zack's friend Jacob standing there with his parents. The children had made their 10 x 12 masterpieces out of colored paper. Above them was a sign that read *When I grow up I'm going to be...*

Zack pointed to his creation. "My teacher couldn't guess."

"Really?" Mitch's brows lifted in surprise. "Anyone can see you're going to be a master spy. That's a cool-looking walkie-talkie you put in there."

Jacob squinted at Zack's picture, then stared at Mitch. "Who's that?" he whispered.

"I'm Mitch. Who are you?"

"Jacob."

"I've heard about you. You're Zack's friend. He and I ride bikes together and play spy."

"I can ride a bike."

"Maybe you could come with us some time," Mitch said.

"He'll need a walkie-talkie."

Mitch winked at Zack. "That can be arranged."

At this juncture Heidi introduced him to Jacob's mom and dad. Then her parents came over to say they had to leave. "Maybe we'll see you sometime," her mother teased quietly.

"Don't be silly. We'll walk you out. Come on, Zack."

"Okay. See ya, Jacob."

The five of them exited the building. After they'd talked a little longer, her parents got in their car and drove off.

Zack looked up at Mitch. "Where's your car?"

"I don't have one. I came here straight from the air-port in a taxi."

Heidi was still reeling from the fact that he'd come at all, that he was back in Salt Lake. "Where's your luggage?"

"I tipped the driver extra to take it to my apartment and leave it in the carport."

"We'll drive you home, huh, Mom," Zack said matter-of-factly.

Mitch sent her a questioning glance. "Will that be all right with you?"

"Of course," she said, opening her car so she wouldn't launch herself into his arms in front of her son. Everyone got in.

"Do you have plans for the rest of the day?" Mitch asked.

"No," Zack spoke up from the backseat as she drove the car out of the parking lot. "Mom says we've got a lot of stuff to do because we have to go on a trip tomorrow."

Mitch's dark eyes practically impaled her. "For how long?" Maybe she was mistaken, but she thought he sounded disappointed. He'd obviously come back to Salt Lake to see about his apartment and have his things shipped to Tallahassee.

She swallowed hard. "We need a vacation, so we're going to visit Evy in Kimball, Nebraska, for the next three weeks. I think I told you she had a baby recently."

"Are you going to fly?"

"No, drive. I like driving."

"But it's going to take a long time to get there," Zack grumbled.

Mitch looked back at him. "That's half the fun." When her son didn't respond, he said, "I'm thinking of going on a vacation myself."

She gripped the steering wheel tighter. "Do you mean before you go back to Florida?"

"Heidi, there's something you need to know. I resigned my job as a federal marshal. Lew took it a lot better than I thought he would. I'm making Salt Lake my permanent home."

"You are?" Zack cried out in pure joy.

The news was so completely unexpected, she almost ran into the back of his car and had to stomp on the brakes to prevent a collision. "I—I don't understand."

"Come inside and I'll explain."

Zack scrambled out of the car ahead of them, whooping it up. Heidi entered the apartment on legs weak as jelly. Mitch brought up the rear, picking up his suitcase on the way inside. She grabbed onto the kitchen counter while he got a can of lemonade out of the fridge for Zack.

"Can I go in your mini-gym? I promise not to spill this."

"Go ahead. The dumbbells are all yours."

"Yay." He dashed out of the kitchen.

With that taken care of, Mitch turned to her. Their gazes clung. "What about the hope that your mother or father will come looking for you one day?"

He shook his head. "That's no longer my priority. As a very wise man said to me, they did their job by giving me life. Now it's my job to live it fully."

"Oh, Mitch…" She couldn't see him clearly because of the tears.

"I love Salt Lake. I love the friends I've made here. I love my job. Most of all, I love you. I fell totally in love with you the first day we met. I loved everything about you. I remember thinking that if I could ever win the love of a woman like you, I wouldn't ask another thing of life. You're the prize every man dreams of."

"I felt the same about you!" she cried.

"The next day I met Zack. That special feeling happened again. He crawled right into my heart and has been in there ever since. I want to marry you, Heidi. I want you to be my wife. I want Zack to be my son. I want to put roots down with you, the kind Saska Bauer put down when she came here. Would you be willing to risk spending the rest of your life with me?"

She was having trouble believing this was really happening. "Before you came to the program," she said. "I was terrified I would have to try and make it through the rest of my life without you. I couldn't imagine it."

The lines in his handsome face relaxed. "That's all I needed to hear. How would you feel about a wedding while you're on vacation? For convention's sake I'm willing to wait another week, maybe. The truth is, I've been waiting for you to come along for years and I don't want to wait any longer. That is, if you'll have me."

"If I'll have you…"

Mad with joy, she ran into his arms. He let out an exultant cry and carried her into the living room, following her down on the couch while their mouths sought to appease their deep hunger for each other. "I couldn't live without you now, Mitch," she confessed when he let her up for breath.

"You don't have to. I'm all yours."

Heidi was so besotted, she forgot everything until later when she heard Zack's voice. He'd come in the living room and was standing next to the couch. The knowledge that he'd caught them like this brought the blood rushing to her face.

"I've been spying on you. Hey, Mitch? Are you really getting married?"

She felt her husband-to-be's kiss on her neck before he sat up.

"What do you think?" Zack let out a yelp of joy as Mitch pulled him down with them.

Chapter Eleven

Seven weeks later

Mitch was just getting ready to leave the office and drive home when his cell phone rang. He checked the caller ID. It was Morton, Heidi's attorney. She and Mitch had met with him right before their wedding a month ago. He clicked on. "This is Mitch Garrett."

"Hello, Mr. Garrett," a brisk female voice said. "Mr. Morton knows it's late in the day, but he wanted to know if you have time to speak to him for a moment."

"Of course."

"Just a minute, please."

Mitch clutched his phone tighter, wondering if this call had anything to do with Heidi's ex-husband. Gary's jury trial was coming up next week.

"Hello, Mitch. Thanks for taking my call. How's marriage treating you so far?"

Mitch closed his eyes tightly. "If there were words, I would tell you."

"That's wonderful. I'm calling because I have some news that might add to your speechless state. The adoption went through when your marriage documents were filed. Judge Rampton is a close friend of

Heidi's father—that helped speed up the process. Congratulations. You now have a son with the legal name Zackery Bauer Garrett."

"Thank you," he murmured, barely able to contain his joy.

"My secretary tried to reach your wife, but there was no answer and no way to leave a message."

"I'm glad she couldn't. Now I can surprise Heidi myself."

When he disconnected, he was already out the door headed for his car. After he and Heidi had made slow, leisurely love this morning, she'd said she was planning to fix him Wiener schnitzel for dinner. It was a favorite Austrian family recipe she'd promised he was going to love.

Heidi didn't need to promise him anything. He was so in love with her he didn't know a man could be this happy. Lew had flown out for their small church wedding and had taken him aside. "Do you remember the times you told me you weren't cut out for marriage?"

Mitch remembered. In truth he'd been glad he'd almost given up on love ever happening to him. For the prize that awaited him, he had to get shot first. And then he had to get sent to Salt Lake for rehabilitation. And then Roman had to give him one last case to work on. And then Heidi Norris Bauer had to walk through the door of his office.

An adorable, voluptuous, grown-up, intelligent woman with cherublike golden hair and jewel-blue eyes. A tough little blue-eyed Marine as part of the package. His family now, legally and forever.

His pulse hammered in his ears as he pulled into the driveway. "Darling?" he called out, hurrying through the house. A wonderful aroma greeted him from the kitchen, but she wasn't in there. No sounds of Zack, either. He dashed down the hall to their bedroom.

Heidi was just coming out of their bathroom with a towel fastened around her. He'd long since discovered that lemony fragrance came from her shampoo. Finding her fresh from the shower was like finding the pot of gold at the end of the rainbow. She let out a cry of delighted surprise when she saw him.

"What perfect timing." He lifted her and carried her to the bed, then lay her there and followed her down. It was pure heaven to bury his face in her curls; it was like lying in a high sunny meadow of flowers. "Where's our son?"

"He's at Jacob's. They're having hot dogs and his parents will bring him home later."

He gave her a long, hard kiss. "I'm going to take a quick shower. Wait for me."

HE NEVER NEEDED TO ASK. She was his wife, and no wife had ever been more loved or felt more cherished. Marriage to this man had made her feel reborn. Tonight she had a secret she was going to share with him over dinner, but maybe she'd do it now. At least that's what she'd thought until she saw him emerge from the shower. Then every thought was put on hold as she reached out to embrace him.

Phyllis had called him a gorgeous hunk. He was that and so much more. Every time he touched her as a prelude to making love, it was like the first time, filling her with rapture. Her need for him would have been embarrassing if he didn't reveal the same great need for her.

They lost track of time giving each other pleasure. When she came back down to earth, she said, "I'm so deeply in love with you it scares me it might be too much for you."

He covered her face with kisses. "Don't be silly. Would you feel any better if I told you the adoption came through? Zack is now my son *officially.*"

"This soon?" she cried in disbelief.

"Mr. Morton tried to get you on the phone. He reached me as I was leaving the office and told me."

"Oh, Mitch—" she sighed "—this is the best news. From now on Zack can call himself Zack Garrett. In case you haven't guessed already, he adores you."

"The feeling's mutual."

She traced the line of his compelling mouth with her finger. "I think only one more piece of news could top this red-letter day."

He blinked.

"Because I know you so well, I can't keep back what I was planning to tell you over dinner."

"What?" His voice shook.

Staring into those dark beautiful eyes of his, she said, "Certain symptoms are showing up that make me pretty sure we're going to have a baby. When we decided we didn't want to wait a long time to have another child, the heavens must have heard us. But I haven't made an appointment with the doctor yet."

She felt the sensation that passed through his body. *"Heidi..."* His elation electrified her. "Have you done a home pregnancy test?"

"No. I thought we'd do it together."

He rubbed his hand over her flat stomach. She knew

how he felt. To think a new life had been formed. A miracle. "I hope my lovemaking didn't hurt you."

Tears of love glazed her eyes. "Of course not."

She could see him swallowing hard. "Have you bought a kit?"

"It's in the bathroom cupboard. Shall we find out now?" He acted like a man who'd gone into shock. She grabbed the towel and slid off the bed. "I'll be right back. Wait for me," she mimicked his earlier words.

"This man's not going anywhere."

A minute later she came out in her bathrobe, saw him sitting on the bed dressed in T-shirt and shorts and showed him the test results. "What does it say?"

He took it from her, but his hand was shaking. "It's positive."

"I knew it. I should have had my period last week."

Mitch looked up at her in wonder. "We're going to have a baby."

"Yes, darling." She sat on his lap and looped her arms around his neck. "Now you've really put down roots. If it's a girl, what do you want to call her?"

"That's easy, but only if you like it, too."

She kissed his hard jaw. "Tell me."

"Saska."

"Really?" His choice thrilled her. "The family will be overjoyed, especially Bruno."

"Do you remember my telling you about the conversation with the priest in Florida?"

"I haven't forgotten anything."

He crushed her to him. "When he was talking about the thousands of people who crossed the Atlantic to come live in America, he was talking about her. I've wanted to claim her for my ancestor ever since."

By now Heidi was beyond happy. "And what if it's a boy?"

"Why don't we discuss it with Zack while we eat that fabulous Wiener schnitzel. I think I just heard the front door open."

"Mom?"

Her husband had the ears of a bloodhound. "In the bedroom, honey."

"Where's Mitch?"

"I don't know any Mitch," she called, teasing.

Zack appeared in the doorway. "Yes, you do. He's right there."

"Oh…you mean this guy?" She kissed Mitch's cheek. "I guess you can keep calling him Mitch if you want to, but he has another name now."

"What?"

"You know how you've kept wishing he were your real dad?"

Zack nodded.

"Well, today you got your wish. The judge granted the adoption. You're now officially *his,* son."

The blue eyes grew huge. "Honest?"

"Cross my heart, honey."

"As of today, your name is Zackery Bauer Garrett. How do you like it?" Mitch asked in a husky voice.

"I can call you Daddy?" Zack's voice came out like a squeak.

"I've been waiting to hear it. Come here, son."

* * * * *

HEART & HOME

COMING NEXT MONTH
AVAILABLE MAY 8, 2012

#1401 A CALLAHAN WEDDING
Callahan Cowboys
Tina Leonard

#1402 LASSOING THE DEPUTY
Forever, Texas
Marie Ferrarella

#1403 THE COWBOY SHERIFF
The Teagues of Texas
Trish Milburn

#1404 THE MAVERICK RETURNS
Fatherhood
Roz Denny Fox

REQUEST YOUR FREE BOOKS!
2 FREE NOVELS PLUS 2 FREE GIFTS!

♦ **Harlequin**®

American ★ *Romance*®

LOVE, HOME & HAPPINESS

YES! Please send me 2 FREE Harlequin® American Romance® novels and my 2 FREE gifts (gifts are worth about $10). After receiving them, if I don't wish to receive any more books, I can return the shipping statement marked "cancel." If I don't cancel, I will receive 4 brand-new novels every month and be billed just $4.49 per book in the U.S. or $5.24 per book in Canada. That's a saving of at least 14% off the cover price! It's quite a bargain! Shipping and handling is just 50¢ per book in the U.S. and 75¢ per book in Canada.* I understand that accepting the 2 free books and gifts places me under no obligation to buy anything. I can always return a shipment and cancel at any time. Even if I never buy another book, the two free books and gifts are mine to keep forever.

154/354 HDN FEP2

Name _____ (PLEASE PRINT)

Address _____ Apt. #

City _____ State/Prov. _____ Zip/Postal Code

Signature (if under 18, a parent or guardian must sign)

Mail to the **Reader Service:**
IN U.S.A.: P.O. Box 1867, Buffalo, NY 14240-1867
IN CANADA: P.O. Box 609, Fort Erie, Ontario L2A 5X3

Not valid for current subscribers to Harlequin American Romance books.

Want to try two free books from another line?
Call 1-800-873-8635 or visit www.ReaderService.com.

* Terms and prices subject to change without notice. Prices do not include applicable taxes. Sales tax applicable in N.Y. Canadian residents will be charged applicable taxes. Offer not valid in Quebec. This offer is limited to one order per household. All orders subject to credit approval. Credit or debit balances in a customer's account(s) may be offset by any other outstanding balance owed by or to the customer. Please allow 4 to 6 weeks for delivery. Offer available while quantities last.

Your Privacy—The Reader Service is committed to protecting your privacy. Our Privacy Policy is available online at www.ReaderService.com or upon request from the Reader Service.

We make a portion of our mailing list available to reputable third parties that offer products we believe may interest you. If you prefer that we not exchange your name with third parties, or if you wish to clarify or modify your communication preferences, please visit us at www.ReaderService.com/consumerschoice or write to us at Reader Service Preference Service, P.O. Box 9062, Buffalo, NY 14269. Include your complete name and address.

HAR11B

*After a bad decision—or two—Annie Mendes
is determined to succeed as a P.I. But her first assignment
could be her last, because one thing is clear: she's not cut
out to be a nanny. And Louisiana detective Nate Dufrene
seems to know there's more to her than meets the eye!*

*Read on for an exciting excerpt of the upcoming book
WATERS RUN DEEP by Liz Talley...*

THE SOUND OF A CAR behind her had Annie scooting off the
road and checking over her shoulder.

Nate Dufrene.

Her heart took on a galloping rhythm that had nothing to
do with exercise.

He slowed beside her. "Wanna ride?"

"I'm almost there. Besides, I wouldn't want to get your
seat sweaty."

His gaze traveled down her body before meeting her
eyes. Awareness ignited in her blood. "I don't mind."

Her mind screamed, *get your butt back to the house and
leave Nate alone.* Her libido, however, told her to take the
candy he offered and climb into his car like a naughty little
girl. Damn, it was hard to ignore candy like him.

"If you don't mind." She pulled open the door and
climbed inside.

The slight scent of citrus cologne, which suited him,
filled the car. She inhaled, sucking in cool air and Nate.
Both were good.

"You run often?" he asked.

"Three or four times a week."

"Oh, yeah? Maybe we can go for a run together."

Her body tightened unwillingly as thoughts of other
things they could do together flitted through her mind. She

shrugged as though his presence wasn't affecting her. Which it *so* was. Lord, what was wrong with her? *He* wasn't her assignment.

"Sure." No way—not if she wanted to keep her job. As he parked, she reached for the door handle, but his hand on her arm stopped her. His touch was warm, even on her heated flesh.

"What did you say you were before becoming a nanny?"

Alarm choked out the weird sexual energy that had been humming in her for the past few minutes. Maybe meeting him on the road wasn't as coincidental as it first seemed. "A real-estate agent."

Will Nate discover Annie's secret?
Find out in WATERS RUN DEEP by Liz Talley,
available May 2012 from Harlequin® Superromance®.

And be sure to look for the other two books
in Liz's THE BOYS OF BAYOU BRIDGE series,
available in July and September 2012.

Harlequin *Presents*®

Royalty has never been so scandalous!

THE
SANTINA
CROWN

When Crown Prince Alessandro of Santina proposes
to paparazzi favorite Allegra Jackson it promises
to be *the* social event of the decade!

Harlequin Presents® invites you to step into the decadent
playground of the world's rich and famous and rub shoulders
with royalty, sheikhs and glamorous socialites.

**Collect all 8 passionate tales written by *USA TODAY*
bestselling authors, beginning May 2012!**